A WHISKER OF DANGER

A WHISKERS AND WORDS MYSTERY
BOOK SIX

ERYN SCOTT

KRISTOPHERSON
PRESS
Publishing

Finding a body in your garden center is kind of a big *dill*.

It's grand opening time for Willow's nursery. Louisa's best friend is brimming with nerves, sure something's going to go wrong. It doesn't help that her beloved pygmy goat, Steve, has recently gone missing. To make matters worse, on the morning of her first day of business, Willow shows up to find her front gate wide open. She should be worried if anything has been stolen, but she's more concerned with the body lying cold in the middle of the succulents.

When the victim is identified as an auditor for the Department of Agriculture with documentation showing Willow was in possession of plants prohibited for sale in the state, the local police look at her as their prime suspect. Willow, distraught, swears the auditor was mistaken. With a little digging, Lou discovers that Willow wasn't the only one to have issues with the deceased man. It looks like they'll have to venture into Brine, the pickle-themed town next door to find allies if they have any hope of proving Willow's innocence.

Welcome to Button

1 - Whiskers and Words   4 - George's Technology Emporium   7 - Button Bistro

2 - Material Girls   5 - Bean and Button Coffeehouse   8 - Pet Store   9 - Bakery

3 - Willow and Easton's houses   6 - The Upholstered Button   10- Old Mansion

11- Willow's Nursery   12- Scoop O' Button

CHAPTER 1

Louisa Henry placed her hands flat on the marble countertops in her best friend Willow's kitchen. The cool stone grounded her and stopped her fingers from shaking. She needed to compose herself; it wouldn't help Willow if she started freaking out too.

"This is horrible, awful, terrible, the worst. Of all the days..." Willow circled the kitchen island, her right hand plastered to her forehead as if she were trying the same grounding technique Lou was using with the countertops.

Though she had control of her shaking hands now, Lou opened her mouth and found she still didn't know what to say. This really *was* terrible timing. Today was supposed to be all about Willow's lifelong dream of opening her own nursery. The last thing she needed was to lose her beloved pet pygmy goat, Steve.

Lou had awoken to a frantic call from her best friend. At first, Lou had assumed there was some emergency with the nursery. They'd worked all evening—staying until the sun had set last night—making sure everything was ready for the grand opening. Still, as a business owner herself, Lou knew things could always go wrong.

But Willow hadn't been calling about a nursery crisis. She'd gone to feed Steve and OC, the chestnut gelding who made up the other half of Willow's pet world, only to find OC agitated and alone. And although the two had a penchant for escaping, they always worked together. Steve had never left on his own.

Which was partly why Lou had such a bad feeling in her gut. She wasn't sure the word "lost" accurately described what had happened to Steve. "Taken" seemed a lot more possible.

Out the kitchen window, OC still paced around his paddock, throwing his head in frustration now and then. Willow mirrored her horse's movements as she marched back and forth through her kitchen—her version of the equine head toss was the constant side-to-side shaking of her head.

"Are you sure he didn't escape again?" Ramona, Willow's mother, asked from where she was perched on the edge of the couch in Willow's living room.

Willow dropped her hand from where it had been flattened to her forehead. "I didn't find any holes in the fence. And he hasn't broken out in weeks."

The pygmy goat, initially purchased to keep the wily OC entertained so he would stop breaking out of his paddock and wandering into the neighbor's yard, had turned out to be even more of an escape artist than his equine counterpart. But that had become less of an issue since Willow and her neighbor, a local detective named Easton West, had begun dating. Steve and OC had slowed their efforts to escape almost immediately, as if they realized it wasn't having the same exasperating impact.

"I think we should go drive around again," Willow's dad said, standing to his full height. He plucked a mesh hay bag from the arm of the couch—Willow must've set it there in her haste that morning—and said, "Is this his leash?" He pinched at the edges, opening it up to its full width, and frowned.

Ramona stood, too, almost as tall as her husband. It was no wonder Willow was so tall. Both her parents were well over average height. She placed a hand on her husband's arm. "No, Joel honey. That's the horse's leash," she whispered incorrectly. "Maybe Willow has some … granola? Chocolate chips? What do goats eat? We could lure him back."

Willow blinked at her parents, obviously too overwhelmed to answer their wildly off base questions. It was a wonder that she was good with animals and plants at all, given those two. Ramona was a classically trained French chef, so long hours at her restaurant meant pets were never an option in her life. And Joel was a military man who held the opinion that plants and animals only created messes.

Her upbringing made Willow even more impressive to Lou. She'd not only developed the greenest thumb of anyone Lou had ever met, despite growing up around fake plants, but she was great with animals. She didn't just have a strong bond with OC and Steve but was also wonderful with the cats who lived in Lou's bookshop down the street. And there were a lot of them.

Whiskers and Words was a rescue-cat sanctuary, besides being a bookstore and a cozy home for Lou and her deaf cat, Sapphire.

Seeing her friend needed help, Lou walked over to Joel. "That's a feed bag," she said gently, taking it from Willow's father. "And Easton's out searching. I think the best thing we can do right now is to wait for him to return."

As if she'd conjured him, Easton shut the front door and walked into the kitchen. Willow locked eyes with her significant other in question.

He shook his head, his blue eyes pained as he took in Willow's agitated state. "I drove through town three times." Seeing Willow wilt at the news, he added, "But I have patrols going nonstop for the next few hours."

Joel snorted next to Lou and muttered, "An excellent use of the police force."

His snarky attitude didn't surprise her. Joel and Easton had been butting heads like two goats themselves since Willow's parents had arrived yesterday to help with opening-day preparations.

Despite the tension, Lou pressed her lips into a line to stop herself from smiling at the man's comment about the police force. If he only knew. Two days ago, the entire Button police force had spent hours wrangling a bunch of ducklings who'd wandered into the middle of town.

The town's first—and only—rideshare driver had narrowly missed the fluffy-feathered crew during her inaugural drive. Martie had been taking Mrs. Jensen to the local pharmacy to fill a prescription for eye drops, her brand new Ryde sign displayed clearly in her van's windshield, when she'd come to a screeching halt in the middle of Stitch Street. It had been quite the scene, and having the local officers there had helped keep everyone calm.

Lou supposed it *was* beneath the police officers' skill level, but Lou preferred them to have jobs like that to focus on instead of thefts and murders, matters their small town had experienced too frequently as of late.

"Willow, I think what we need to do is get you over to the nursery," Easton said, placing a gentle hand on her shoulder. "That'll help distract you for the day. I promise we'll find him."

Willow wrapped her arms around Easton, holding him tight as if he was now the thing keeping her grounded.

Lou remembered the feeling of having someone to lean on. Her late husband, Ben, had been that for her as well. And even though a hug couldn't erase problems, Lou knew that the embrace of the right person could do wonders for making problems seem manageable.

The missing goat aside, Lou's heart soared at seeing her friend so happy in her relationship. Unlike Willow's parents, Lou was of the opinion that Willow and Easton were perfectly matched.

"We can drive Willow to the nursery." Joel stepped forward, addressing the tall detective. "Why don't you join your officers and continue the search?"

A sadness flashed behind Easton's eyes. Lou was sure he wanted to be there with Willow during her opening day. He'd been eating, sleeping, and dreaming nursery business right alongside Willow over the past few months after all. Yesterday, when they were taking care of last-minute preparations, Easton had even taken to parroting some of Willow's same lines, like the dangers of leaving the hoses unattended: "A customer could trip." Or using the forbidden blast setting on the spray nozzles: "It's just going to blast all the topsoil out of the planter." But he nodded, his throat bobbing as he swallowed the reality that Willow's dad was right. Searching for Steve was the best place for him to be.

Willow stepped back from their hug and grabbed Easton's hand, squeezing it tight. "Thank you. Knowing you're out there definitely gives me the most peace of mind." With one last look over her shoulder at OC, Willow followed her parents out the front door.

Outside, Easton climbed into his truck, splitting off from the group as he backed up and drove down the shared driveway between his and Willow's houses.

Despite her underlying worry about Steve, Lou couldn't help but feel her excitement surge as she climbed into her car and followed Willow's parents' SUV as they drove toward the other side of town. She couldn't wait to see the gorgeous nursery full of happy customers. Valley Nursery was officially Lou's new favorite place to be, if you didn't count her cozy bookstore full of cats.

Based on how slowly the vehicle in front of her was moving, Lou wasn't alone in scanning the side streets and underbrush along the lanes and avenues of the small town as she drove, hoping to glimpse a small, wiry gray goat chomping on a lush bit of spring grass.

Unfortunately, there were no Steve sightings on the trip across town. Peggy Lee's truck was already waiting in the nursery parking lot when they arrived. There was another car as well, one Lou didn't recognize, but she didn't have time to consider whose it might be, because something else stole her focus. It seemed to capture everyone's attention based on the open mouths and wrinkled brows of Willow's parents as they exited the vehicle and walked up to the gated entrance to the nursery.

An eight-foot carved wooden troll holding a giant watering can stood just to the right of the entrance. He wore blue overalls and big green clogs. His dry-looking troll skin was painted a cedar-bark brownish red. His giant nose, huge ears, bald head, and enormous jaw were all carved in detail, as were his sad blue eyes.

"What is that?" Ramona covered her mouth with her hand as she gawked at her daughter.

Willow blinked, stunned. It was clear she had no more of an idea than anyone else in the party.

"Pick your jaws up off the floor, people," a gruff voice called from behind them as a truck door slammed shut. Peggy Lee, Willow's ornery but lovable business partner, ambled toward them. "That's ValNur the troll. Happy opening day." Even though it was supposed to be an exclamation, Peggy Lee's tone remained rather flat, and she only raised her arms up a few inches as she gestured toward the carved troll.

Behind Peggy Lee, a hulking young man quietly hung back. Beau Frazier worked on the farm where Peggy Lee lived, and where they'd spent the last six months growing the stock that now sat inside the fenced area of Valley Nursery.

"ValNur? ValNur," Willow said, repeating the name. Lou wasn't sure if she was trying to get used to it or if she was just in shock, caught in a repetitive loop.

"Get it?" Beau said. "Valley Nursery. Val-Nur."

The group let out a collective "ah." Peggy Lee huffed. "It's not like it's some difficult word puzzle. Benji carved him for me years ago, and I've never found a good place for him until now."

"And how did you decide *this* is where he needed to be?" Willow asked in a strangled tone.

Peggy Lee scowled. "He's good luck. You'll see. People will love him."

An awkward silence fell over the group. Peggy Lee's husband had passed away five years ago, and she'd become quite reclusive until Willow had convinced her to partner with her in the nursery venture. No one wanted to be the one to mention that Peggy Lee's late husband's carving was rather grotesque.

Willow checked her watch. "Okay, well, we have an hour until opening. We've got a lot to do. Let's get—" Willow's voice cut out as she stepped over to the chain-link fence that ran the perimeter of her nursery, keeping people out and her beloved plants inside between business hours.

She bent down to pick up something from the concrete. In her hand lay the heavy-duty lock she'd splurged on to keep everything secured. It had been cut, the metal peeling back as if it was merely a piece of clay that had been snipped with scissors from a kitchen drawer.

"Peggy Lee, have you been inside yet?" Willow's eyes were round as they flashed over to her business partner.

The older woman grunted. "No. Beau and I dropped off ValNur and then went to grab breakfast. I didn't even think to check the lock."

Fingers shaking, Willow pulled the fence open and rushed inside, scanning the place as if cataloging each plant, each pot, and making sure nothing was missing. After the amount of time she'd spent at the place over the past few months, she probably *did* have everything on the property memorized.

Lou practically did too. And her heartbeat slowed as she walked inside; it didn't look like anything had been taken.

The indoor plants, housed in the first and only internally heated greenhouse, were all lined up or hanging just where they had been yesterday when Lou had left. The section Lou had helped organize, full of ornamental miniatures one could add to their potted plants to create a whimsical forest scene or fairy house, hadn't been touched either. While the water in the fountains next to that remained calm since no one had turned on the power to them yet, all the pumps and water-feature supplies were where they were supposed to be.

Following Willow, Lou sped into an open-air greenhouse, full of vegetable starts. Footsteps behind them told her the group was trailing after. The bright green seedlings shooting up out of rich, dark soil seemed to settle Willow because her footsteps became steadier as she entered the next greenhouse.

But when Willow stopped cold in the succulents, Lou's stomach dropped.

"What is it?" Lou asked, approaching her friend quickly at first, and then slowly.

Willow stared at a man lying in the middle of the succulent display Lou had worked so hard on the day prior. His eyes were open, but his body was completely still.

"Who is he?" Lou asked.

"This isn't going to be good." Willow gulped.

Cries and gasps sounded behind them, proving the rest of the group had caught up.

Willow's father was already calling 9-1-1, and Peggy Lee was confirming that the man was, in fact, dead, so Louisa focused on taking care of her friend. She pulled Willow away from the dead man and asked, "What do you mean?"

"Um … I may have just had a pretty heated argument with that man the other day." Willow's eyes darted around the place, as if she were searching for an exit this time rather than checking if anything was missing from her stock.

Lou's mouth sprang open in surprise. "You know who that is?" She shot a wary glance over at the man lying prone next to them.

Swallowing, Willow met Lou's gaze. "That's Harley Bramble. He's the Lakeside County auditor for the Washington State Department of Agriculture, and he was threatening to shut down the nursery."

CHAPTER 2

Lou swayed on her feet. The dizzying number of plants around her made it seem like the world was tilting. But it was the secret her friend had just divulged that truly had her feeling off-balance.

She grabbed on to Willow's arm, whispering, "Willow, you didn't do something illegal, did you?" Lou hated the question as soon as it came out of her mouth, but Willow's words had been so ominous.

Pulling her arm away, Willow complained, "Louuu." It was an entire sentence stuffed inside one word. "Of course I didn't. The guy was paranoid. I mean, in addition to not believing that I'd grown all of my stock which led to him accusing me of not following the proper quarantine periods for certain varietals, he said he needed to test for root rot before I could open even though I assured him my plants were healthy."

"Root rot?" Lou wrinkled her nose. "That's against the law?"

She was pretty sure the sad houseplant she was trying to nurse back to life in the front window of the bookshop had that, and she hadn't gotten any visits from the Department of Agriculture.

Willow shrugged. "It *can* be terrible if it spreads, so I understand why he wants to be vigilant. That's why I called him last night and asked him to meet me here. I was finally going to consent to the testing if it meant I could open on time. But he never showed."

In different circumstances, Lou would've chuckled at her friend's stubborn, hotheaded attitude. Fighting with a state agriculture auditor because she didn't think he was right to question the quality of her stock was something that could've become a funny tale they might've told at the nursery's ten-year anniversary. But Willow was right. This didn't look good for her.

"Well, he showed." Lou grimaced over at the body. "And I'm guessing that was his car parked out in the lot when we arrived." Noticing that she was stressing out her friend, Lou added, "But don't worry. Easton will figure it out."

Just as she said that, a car pulled into the nursery parking lot, sending a wave of relief over Lou ... all of which disappeared when she realized it was a black, unmarked sedan instead of Easton's familiar truck. The man who climbed out wore a scowl as noticeable as the badge he wore on a chain around his neck. His eyes scanned the garden center from under dark eyebrows that matched the shock of black hair on his head.

Willow groaned. "Not Roy." Just like when she'd said

Lou's name moments before, Roy's name seemed to hold so much meaning as it left her. Her shoulders sank forward, and her tense posture slumped in defeat.

Detective Roy Anderson was Button's only other detective. Unlike Easton, he wasn't a single bit charming or kind. Well, Lou had recently seen a softer side of the man. At the end of their last case, Lou felt an unspoken agreement form between the two, centered on mutual respect.

She was banking on that esteem having remained intact as she stepped forward to meet him.

"Detective Anderson," Lou said, dipping her chin in greeting. "Thank you for coming so quickly."

His narrowed gaze cut from Lou to Willow, then back again. "I was the only one not out searching for a lost pet." His tone was almost as sharp as his glare. "Which, now I'm wondering wasn't some sort of ruse to focus the town's police force elsewhere while a man was murdered." His attention fell on the man lying in front of him.

Okay, so maybe that respect wasn't as solid as Lou had thought.

"Excuse you," Ramona blurted out, arms crossed.

Joel took a step closer to the detective. "What makes you think you can come in here and accuse my daughter of something like that?"

Unfazed by the tall military man staring him down, Roy shot a bored look at Joel and knelt next to the body. His eyes pored over the text of the paper stuck to a clipboard near the dead man. "He was going to shut Willow down for violating Washington Administrative Code 16-752-600. Want to know which one that is?" Roy cocked an eyebrow.

Joel folded his arms. "I'm sure you're going to tell us."

"Buying, selling, or trading noxious weeds and-or prohibited plant species."

"What?" Willow stepped forward. "I don't have any prohibited plants here."

Peggy Lee huffed. "What'd you say about my plants?" She gritted her teeth. "I promise you, there aren't noxious weeds on my property. We grew everything right here in the valley."

Standing and pressing his lips forward for a moment, Roy shook his head. "According to that citation, the two of you were being fined for being in the possession of and attempting to sell poison hemlock, tansy ragwort, scotch broom, as well as"—Roy's glare deepened as he added— "the highly toxic manchineel tree."

Willow gasped. Everyone else present blinked in confusion, not sure what that was.

"That thing can make you sick if you so much as touch it," Willow snapped out at Roy. "Why would I have one in my nursery?"

Peggy Lee nodded. "Yeah." She frowned at Willow. "What is it exactly?"

But instead of letting Willow answer, Roy said, "Pretty much every part of a manchineel tree can either kill you or cause severe damage. Their sap causes boils." He eyed the red welts on the dead man's hands. "If you burn them, the ash can cause respiratory failure. Even standing under one of them during a rainstorm can lead to burns on the skin." When Willow arched her eyebrow in question, Roy added, "My grandparents used to live down in the Florida Keys. I learned all about the manchineel from them."

"Why would we have a tree as dangerous as that in a place of business?" Peggy Lee asked.

Ignoring the older woman's question, Roy donned gloves, knelt, and gently touched the man's chin, causing his mouth to open. "And while I'll wait until the medical examiner has his say, I'd bet that small apple is also from a manchineel tree and is going to be our cause of death."

Lou couldn't help but notice that besides the rashes on the dead man's hands, his eyes were also rimmed in red, the skin seeming to have been irritated as well. The other thing that caught her attention was a small zigzagged silver chain of folded gum wrappers, like Lou and Willow used to make back in middle school. It was about three inches long and at least a foot away from the body. Roy caught her staring and knelt over, putting the chain into an evidence bag while he still wore his gloves.

Tires screeched to a halt in the parking lot. No less than three police cruisers followed Easton's truck. He beat the uniformed officers inside, his long legs eating up the familiar ground of the nursery.

"I came as soon as I heard the call." He huffed, breathing hard from running. His attention landed on the dead man, causing him to wince and look at Willow. "Is that who I think it is?"

Willow shifted her weight uncomfortably, proving she'd told Easton about the disagreement she'd had with the auditor. "Look," she said, addressing Roy. "That man *was* threatening me with fines, and he was talking about not letting me open, but it was all about him being worried about root rot and a case of verticillium wilt going around the valley. It had nothing to do with prohibited plants, toxic or not." She waved her hand around her in a circle. "You can have them check. I don't have any of those plants you listed on my property."

Roy lifted his chin as the uniformed officers gathered around. "Listen up. I need you to look up the following plants and familiarize yourself with how to identify them. Scotch broom, tansy ragwort, poison hemlock, and the manchineel tree. Search every inch of this place." He stirred the air with his finger as he barked out directions. "I need to know if those plants are anywhere on the premises."

The officers split up as they spread out through the rows of plants.

Easton stayed put. Roy cocked an eyebrow at him.

"Detective West." Roy's voice was calm, but it was clear something dangerous bubbled under the surface. "Are you going to assist, or will you become a problem?"

Easton straightened his shoulders. "Roy, you know Willow. She wouldn't do this. Let me take over this investigation."

Laughing, Roy said, "That's not how this works. I was the first on the scene, and the captain will never agree to let you lead when your girlfriend is the prime suspect."

"I'm the prime suspect?" Willow blurted, covering her mouth with her hand. "I promise, I didn't hurt him. We had one conversation last week, and then I was supposed to meet up with him last night, but that's it."

Roy whirled on Willow. "Last night? That seems odd for

a state auditor to conduct business after hours." He pulled out his notebook and jotted down a note.

Cheeks turning red, Willow shifted her weight as if she couldn't get comfortable. "I called him and asked him to come test the soil like he wanted to during his first visit. It was all I could think to do since today was supposed to be our opening day."

"So you were desperate," Roy summarized, writing more in his notebook.

Willow held out a hand. "No. I mean, a little, but he never even showed so I went straight home. Just ask my parents."

Their expressions turned apologetic.

"Well," Willow said, her cheeks turning red. "They were asleep by the time I got back, and they're heavy sleepers but—"

"Stop talking right now, Willow," Easton cut her off.

Roy shot him a scowl, but Easton stared right back.

"If you won't let me be involved, then I can advise her not to talk to you until she has a lawyer present." His gaze flashed over to Willow. "Which we'll work on finding right now." He motioned for her to follow him as he walked away.

"Don't go too far," Roy called after him, then turned his focus on to Lou. "Care to tell me what happened this morning?"

Confident it would only help her friend, Lou said, "We were all with her this morning. Her pet goat went missing, and we've been focused on finding him. When we arrived *together*, the lock on the perimeter gate had been cut, and when we came inside to check if anything had been stolen, we found him."

"Willow was with us the whole time," Joel repeated, having stuck around even though the rest of the group had followed Willow and Easton out toward the parking lot.

Detective Anderson pursed his lips. "This morning, sure. I believe it." He considered the body. "But from the looks of this guy, he's been dead for hours. Was probably killed last night. What time did Willow say she was supposed to meet with him?"

Lou swallowed. "I don't know."

That part was news to her. And although Lou knew for sure her friend had nothing to do with the man's death, she was also aware that Willow not telling anyone about the meeting only added to the suspicion surrounding her.

"Come on, Lou." Joel placed a hand on her shoulder. "Let's join the others."

She followed Willow's dad away from the surly detective. They found the group crowded around Willow, who was leaning against Easton in the parking lot. Ramona stood next to her, rubbing Willow's back.

"Do you have any lawyers in this town, or is it just full of quilters?" Joel asked no one in particular. Then, without waiting for an answer, he pulled out his phone and said, "I'm calling Lee Darcy. He'll know what to do." The tall man stepped away to talk.

Easton squeezed Willow tighter to him. "Or do you want me to call Virginia?" he asked, mentioning the lawyer who lived on Needle Street.

Joel hesitated in his retreat, his jaw set tight as he

stopped scrolling through his contacts and looked to Willow for her decision. Easton surely just meant to help by mentioning Virginia Stokes, a local lawyer. But Joel's reaction proved that he saw it as a challenge, yet another way for the two men to butt heads.

Willow wet her lips. She sent an apologetic grimace toward her father. "I know you really like Lee, and that he helped you with your will, but Virginia is also fantastic, and I like the fact that she's close by."

Joel snorted and walked off. Ramona, who took the decision in stride as if it were a question of using fish that wasn't up to her restaurant's quality or pivoting and changing the menu last minute, nodded resolutely. "I'll go talk to him. He just wants to help."

"I know he does." Willow's mouth pulled into a wan smile. "Please tell him thank you for me."

Once her mom had gone, Willow looked up at Easton and said, "Yes, let's call Virginia. She'll know what to do here."

"I'll take care of that." Easton pulled out his phone.

Lou glanced over at Joel and Ramona talking a few yards away. Joel glared at Easton. Lou wished, for Willow's sake, her father would lighten up a little. She had a terrible feeling that things wouldn't be getting any easier for Willow in the next few hours. She was going to need all the support she could get, and that included having everyone on her side seeing eye to eye.

CHAPTER 3

Virginia Stokes swept into the parking lot a few minutes later. She wore a dark gray power suit that didn't have a wrinkle on it, as if she'd gone through every inch by hand to make sure her appearance was the epitome of put together. The woman exuded confidence and a very pungent sandalwood-based perfume. Lou wondered if the intense smell had some sort of animal kingdom reasoning behind it, as though her victims were so distracted by the scent, they wouldn't realize she was about to strike until she was already at their throats.

The lawyer whisked Willow off to her office, a cute, tiny house parked on the corner of the property, to talk about her rights and come up with a plan.

Along with Virginia came locals and visitors alike, drawn by the police presence and huddling along the sidewalks as they watched the proceedings inside the nursery. A few cars pulled into the lot, expecting the opening day that had been advertised around town, only to be turned away by Willow's parents, who seemed happy for a job. Peggy Lee and Beau had gone home since they had chores to do on the farm.

After a while inside the office, Willow and Virginia emerged. Virginia approached Detective Anderson. Easton and Lou shared a hopeful glance as Roy climbed into his cruiser and Virginia and Willow got into the lawyer's shiny Mercedes, the two cars heading toward the police station. Lou hoped it would be enough.

With Willow taken care of, Easton moved into the nursery to assist his fellow officers in their search of the property. Seeing everyone else relax into jobs around the place, Lou decided she would make herself useful as well.

Ramona and Joel seemed to have the parking lot covered. Lou didn't dare go inside the nursery on the off chance she might impede the crime scene mapping that was happening inside. She must've been hanging around Willow too much lately because her first thought as she watched the officers sweep through the rows of plants in the nursery was to check to make sure no hoses had been left out that could be tripping hazards. She laughed to herself, giving it to Willow that it was a credible fear now that she thought about it.

Those two options out of the question, and knowing one of her superpowers was observation, Lou put her mind to work watching people and picking out details. Maybe the actual killer was nearby, observing to see how the scene played out.

She concentrated on the locals first, those being the easiest to remember. And while she didn't really believe anyone in Button could've killed the man inside the nursery, maybe a few of them had seen something, and she could pass along their names to Roy.

Lou made a list in her mind. Mrs. Weaver had walked by twice with her miniature poodle. Trudy and Marge—local power walkers who did more gossiping than walking—were chatting on the corner, Dennis Stevens kept acting like he was inspecting a crack in the sidewalk next to the nursery, but he wasn't fooling anyone either.

Next, Lou moved on to the people she didn't recognize. A family who'd obviously been to the tulip farms nearby in the valley stopped to whisper and stare as they clutched at a colorful bouquet. A woman with dark hair and even darker sunglasses sat in a shiny black car parked along the other side of the road. She observed the commotion with a cool interest that piqued Lou's curiosity. But before Lou could walk over to talk to her, Ramona called Lou over. Joel was nowhere to be seen, and Ramona's shoulders were tense with worry.

She stood next to a shabby sedan that had pulled into the lot. Unlike the other visitors who'd pulled in, rolled down their windows, heard the place was closed, and backed out of the lot immediately, the man in the sedan got out. He wore khakis and a frown, as well as a brown mop of hair that looked like it was about two weeks past needing a haircut. He held a black clipboard that was almost identical to the one next to Harley Bramble's body in the nursery.

"Here's Lou. She'll know what to tell you," Ramona told

the man, then turned to Lou to give her a warning look. "This man is from the Department of Agriculture."

Lou faltered as she walked toward him. Based on the icy coldness that washed through her body at Ramona's words, Lou was sure her face must've been sickly pale as she feigned a smile.

"David Houston." He held out his hand to shake Lou's. "I'm the auditor for Skagit County."

Lou didn't feel any clearer about why he was there.

Seeming to expect that question as well, David said, "My boss, the director of agriculture for the state, sent me to check up on whether the police needed to speak with our department or had questions I can relay back to her. She regrets not being able to come herself but had some family issues arise this morning just before we got word about Harley's death."

"Oh, right." Lou glanced over her shoulder. "I can show you to one of our local detectives who's standing in for the lead right now."

David dipped his chin in thanks. "That would be great." He followed as she stepped tentatively toward the crime scene.

Out of the corner of her eye, Lou saw Ramona sigh with relief at not having to talk to the government agent any longer.

"Is this your nursery?" David asked as they walked across the parking lot.

Lou shook her head. "It's my best friend's place."

"Oh. I just ask because I'll probably be splitting Harley's

caseload with some of the other auditors, so I might be seeing more of this place soon," he explained.

Lou returned the gesture but didn't know what to say. *That's nice* didn't seem appropriate. Neither did *Okay, well, make sure you're nicer to my friend than the last guy.* So she kept her mouth shut and held her hand out toward Easton as they approached.

"This is Detective West. You can speak with him." Lou stayed back, eyeing the crime scene techs that worked carefully around the plants, inspecting them for clues that might help in the case.

"Thank you," David said, stepping forward.

Lou was about to leave when Easton caught her eye. "I just got a text that Willow's done at the station. Would you go pick her up? Maybe take her home?"

"Sure," Lou said, happy to leave the tense scene. She hightailed it out of the nursery and toward her car, waving to Ramona and Joel.

This time, as she drove through the streets of Button, Lou didn't stop to search for Steve the goat. The realization sent a pang of guilt through her, but with the way the morning had progressed, Steve was now only *one* of Willow's many problems.

Virginia and Willow waited for Lou outside the police station when she pulled up a few minutes later. After hugging Virginia and waving goodbye, Willow climbed into Lou's car. She sank into the passenger seat and closed her eyes, grabbing the seat belt and buckling it by feel as she kept her eyes shut. Lou drove toward Willow's house without a word.

As someone who'd been the object of Detective Anderson's suspicions before, Lou knew how scary it was and how it could seem as though prison was imminent. The knowledge that she hadn't done the crime wasn't enough to ease her mind. She knew innocent people were convicted of crimes all the time.

And while Willow still hadn't said a word once they pulled into Willow's driveway, she could guess that those were some of the same thoughts flowing freely—and dangerously—through her best friend's mind.

"Are my parents okay?" Willow croaked out once Lou put the car into park and turned off the engine. She opened her eyes and looked at Lou.

"They are. They've been helping—" Lou stopped herself before she finished that sentence. Willow didn't need to know that they'd been turning away customers all morning. "Helping a lot," she added, deciding to leave it at that.

Willow unbuckled herself and got out of the car.

Supportive as everyone had been, Lou was glad Willow's house was quiet and empty when they arrived. She slumped onto the couch, staring at the wall. Then, without preamble, Willow stood, walked over and opened the sliding glass door that led out onto her back deck, and walked outside. Lou followed, waiting to see if she was needed like she and Ben used to follow their nieces around when they would come to visit as toddlers: they wanted to give them their independence, but needed to be close by if either stumbled.

Willow strode through her beautiful garden with a purpose, walking toward the paddock at the edge of her flower beds. OC snorted and threw his head in a greeting as he noticed her. She climbed into the paddock with him. Wrapping her arms around his powerful neck, Willow buried her face into his mane and stood there, supported by the enormous animal. He blinked at Lou, remaining as still as she'd seen him in a long time, as if he knew.

Lou hung back, giving her friend a little more space now that she saw she was in excellent hands—well, hooves.

The urge to ask Willow for her *honest three* came up, but Lou pushed it away. While the friends had been using the phrase to check in with each other for decades, this seemed like a time when it wouldn't be helpful. Without asking, Lou could tell her friend was distraught, and she had a feeling it wouldn't help Willow to put a name to those emotions.

Eventually, Willow pulled away from the horse, taking a moment to scratch behind his velvety soft ears and caress his equally soft nose before she stepped back through the fence. Seeing his support services were no longer needed, he trotted off to the other side of the paddock where he'd been munching on his morning flake of hay.

Willow turned back toward Lou, and she sighed.

"Better?" Lou asked.

Willow nodded. "Better."

Neither woman meant *all the way*. There was still too much up in the air to feel completely better, but Willow obviously felt good enough to use words again, which was enough of an improvement for Lou. She could work with that.

"Okay, I'm going to run to the store and grab you some

essentials," Lou said. While Willow hadn't ever been in trouble with the law before, Lou had been by her side through some pretty difficult times, and she knew exactly what would help. "Are you good here with OC for a few minutes?"

"Yep." Willow dipped her head in a nod. "It's my fault," Willow said, stopping Lou before she could leave. "It's … I was right the other day. I jinxed myself."

Lou remembered just the instance her friend was referring to. It had been last week, when everything was falling into place. Willow had sunk onto the couch in Lou's bookshop and said, "I feel like I need to pinch myself." She'd listed the ways her life seemed like a dream: her dream job, a great boyfriend, living in the same town as her best friend again, etc.

"What's this going to mean for the nursery?" Fear flashed in Willow's eyes.

Lou reached forward and grabbed on to her friend's hand, giving it a squeeze. "We'll figure it out. I promise."

Willow pulled her lips into as much of a smile as she could muster. Lou took off, a sick feeling swirling through her gut. She hated to make promises to Willow that she wasn't sure she could deliver on, but it was Willow. Lou would do anything to make things right in her friend's life again.

Hopping into her car, she drove to the store, eager to start on the first step of that plan, which involved a large bag of Sour Patch Kids and some extra-dark chocolate. The dark chocolate was Willow's favorite, but the Sour Patch Kids were important because they made Willow giggle and dance around from the tartness. Even if it was manufactured by sour sugar, Lou longed to see her friend laugh again.

Lou was just perusing the candy aisle when her phone dinged with a message. It was from George. Lou frowned. The tech-savvy twentysomething was one of her bookshop regulars, but she knew Lou was closed for the day for Willow's grand opening.

> I think I need to swing by with Annie
> tonight if you're going to be around.

Heart sinking, Lou knew what that meant. After coming into Whiskers and Words daily for months to visit with the adoptable felines, George had decided she was ready for a cat of her own. But Anne Mice was the third cat George had tried out that week.

Lou understood when George hadn't clicked with Catnip Everdeen. The skittish orange-and-white spotted cat only had eyes for Silas, another one of Lou's regulars. They'd tried it out, just in case Catnip might "come out of her shell" once she was within George's cozy house. But she'd just hid between the big plastic tubs where George stored her techie equipment.

Charles Lickens, the beautiful British Blue that had come to Lou a few months ago during the holiday season, had been a bust too. He hadn't cowered, instead becoming too loud and bossy once he was the only cat in the house.

But Lou had been sure Anne Mice would be the ticket. She was the Mary Poppins of cats—practically perfect in every way. The gray tabby was sweet, quiet, sociable, and just the right amount of cuddly, while still needing her space from time to time. George adored Annie, as she called her, so Lou was immediately confused.

> What went wrong?

George responded right away.

> I honestly think she missed the customers.
> I think she likes the bustle of the
> bookshop. She kept staring at the door,
> waiting for people to enter and pet her. I
> tried to give her a few days, but she just
> seems more depressed. I can't take that
> from her.

Lou understood. Even though George's home doubled as the local Technology Emporium, she didn't have nearly the foot traffic Lou's bookstore saw. It seemed that as much as Lou wanted Anne Mice to find a home of her own, she may have decided she'd already found one.

> I understand. The thing is, I'm not actually
> sure if I'm going to be around tonight.
> Steve is missing, and there's some trouble
> at the nursery.

> Oh! I totally forgot that today was opening
> day for Willow. Sorry to bug you. Trouble?
> Is everything okay?

Lou didn't know how to answer that question. As much as she wanted it to be fine, and had promised her best friend that it would be, she didn't know this time. She also didn't know how much Detective Anderson wanted her spilling to the townspeople though she was sure the police crawling around the place would get the locals' attention.

I don't know. I'll text when I'm home.

George, a woman who'd needed to deal with her own secrets in her own time, didn't push the subject as others may have.

Let me know if there's anything I can do. I can also check on the cats later if you're still busy.

Thanks.

Lou focused on grabbing the last few things from the grocery store. Arms laden with bags of things that she knew would cheer up her best friend, Lou headed back to her car. Though, she had a bad feeling that unless those bags held a gray pygmy goat or the name of the real criminal in Harley's death, they wouldn't do what Willow needed them to do.

WILLOW WAS STILL in the yard when Lou returned. She wasn't in the paddock with OC but had kicked off her shoes and was standing in the cool green grass of her backyard, staring off into the field beyond her training arena.

Sidling up to her friend, Lou gave her a quick side hug.

Willow attempted a smile, but it was as if there wasn't enough happiness inside her to convince the corners of her mouth to pull up. The result was a flat grimace.

"I've got chocolate and other essentials inside," Lou said, adding, "or would you like me to bring them out here?" She studied her friend, waiting to see what she needed at that moment.

"Do you feel like going for a drive? I do. I think driving might be good." Willow turned back toward the house, her long legs taking her much farther and faster than Lou, who jogged to keep up.

"Uh, sure," Lou called, scrambling after her friend.

It was a good thing she hadn't unpacked the snacks yet, because Willow swept through the house, and Lou just had time to snatch the bag off the counter as they moved through the kitchen on their way out to the car.

Lou unlocked her car and climbed into the driver's side, handing the bag of supplies over to Willow. She started the car, backed up, and stopped. Willow turned her attention from the window to Lou, nonverbally asking why she was stopping.

"Where am I driving?" Lou asked.

Willow swallowed, her eyes darting around them. "I don't know," she admitted. "It's just … Steve." With the police at the nursery, no one was out patrolling for the goat.

"Gotcha." Lou didn't need anything more than that.

Willow needed a win today. They needed to find that goat.

CHAPTER 4

Easton sat on Willow's porch when she and Lou returned a few hours later.

The same way that the women's dejected body language immediately communicated their lack of progress in the goat search, Easton communicated that he had no good news to share with them on the nursery front. In fact, the way he flinched as Willow approached told Lou he might even have more bad news.

"What is it?" Willow asked, the question a whine that told Easton she couldn't take much more.

He held up a hand like Willow often did when approaching OC during one of his wild horse playtimes. "You need to eat dinner. I have an idea, and I need you to hear me out."

Willow's expression soured before she even heard what Easton was asking, probably sure if he had to preface it in that way, she wouldn't like it.

"I made plans for us to have dinner with Roy and his new girlfriend in a few hours," he admitted.

Lou frowned. Easton was normally overly attentive with Willow's feelings. After the terrible day, Lou expected Easton to be catering to Willow's every need, not signing her up for an awkward dinner with the man who'd been treating her like she was a murderer.

Despite the calm voice Easton had used, Willow stomped up the porch steps. "Is he sure he wants to have dinner with the 'prime suspect' in the murder he's investigating?" She used angry finger quotes around the words he'd used to describe her back at the nursery.

Easton followed Willow inside. Lou scuttled after.

"Look, I sat down with him just a few minutes ago. I begged him to think about it rationally. He knows you." Easton's throat bobbed as he swallowed. "Then I asked him if there was anything we could do."

Willow and Lou stared at Easton, waiting.

"He brought up the dinner, told me it was his girl-friend's idea and it would mean a lot to him if we came with them. I think it would be smart to show him you're not a killer and remind him he knows you," Easton pleaded as Willow unlocked her door and stormed inside. "But if you think it's a bad idea, I can cancel."

Willow stopped in the kitchen, whirling around on Lou, who stood there with the bag of junk food from the car. Lou peered down at the bag in her hand, much lighter than when they'd entered the car hours earlier.

"It might not be the worst idea," Lou offered. "You've been surviving off junk food and stress for the last few hours, so you would at least get some proper food in you out of the deal."

Easton shot Lou a thankful glance before turning back toward Willow.

"Maybe you're right." Willow let her shoulders drop a few inches from the tense position they'd been in all day. "Who's the girlfriend?" she asked. It was as if the stress had created a fog around Willow's mind that she couldn't see through until she let the air clear. Now that it was, interest seeped from her posture.

But Easton wasn't able to appease her. "I don't know," he said. "He just mentioned that they'd recently started dating and that she was asking him if he and any of the other officers ever do double dates." Easton lifted a shoulder and then let it drop. "Considering most of the station dislikes the guy, I think we're kind of his only option."

Empathy for the man swirled through Lou. As much as Detective Anderson rubbed her the wrong way, especially when he was accusing the people she loved of murder, she caught a sadness in him, buried deep.

"Sure. Let's do it." Willow pushed back her shoulders. "Wait. Where are my parents?" She surveyed the house, as if they might be hiding.

Easton cocked an eyebrow in annoyance. "They came by, and when they saw it was just me, they said they were going to grab something to eat and they'd see you later tonight." He sniffed. "I might've mentioned that we had dinner plans."

Willow nodded, content that she hadn't missed her

parents. They were busy people, and Lou knew their work schedules barely allowed for them to come up for the weekend. "Okay. Lou, want to help me figure out what to wear? What says I didn't kill that man and couldn't ever harm anyone?"

Lou laughed as she followed Willow upstairs to her closet. They chose a sage-green maxi dress that brought out Willow's blue eyes and a cream-colored cardigan in case it got colder once the sun set.

Willow considered her reflection in the mirror. "Okay, I guess here goes nothing."

"It's going to be great." Lou gave her friend an encouraging smile.

"It's terrible," Willow whispered on the phone a few hours later.

Lou readjusted the phone against her ear. It was only five minutes past six. "Already?" she asked with a little chuckle. "It hasn't even been ten minutes."

There was a shuffling sound on the other end of the call, and Willow said, "It was terrible from the first moment, but I figured it would look suspicious if I left right away, so I waited a few minutes. Can you come here? We need a buffer."

Lou looked around. She was sitting on her couch, two and a half cats lying on her. Sapphire was merely resting a paw on her shoulder from where he was perched behind her, so he didn't count as a whole. Her stomach had grumbled over an hour earlier, but she hadn't wanted to get up, lest she disturb the cats. The book she was reading was great, so she'd been content.

But if Willow needed her, she could head out for dinner. "Sure," Lou said, closing her book and slipping it onto the coffee table. She carefully extracted Sapphy's paw from her shoulder, then slid her leg out from under Charles Lickens so he would land on the couch. Anne Mice was another story. She was sprawled across Lou's stomach, as close to her as she could get. She'd been extra clingy ever since George dropped her off.

"Perfect. Easton's texting with Noah right now." Willow's whispered voice kicked up into an excited register.

"N-Noah?" Lou stammered out the name of their friend, the local veterinarian.

Willow scoffed. "When I asked Bella if I could invite a friend, she insisted it be another couple."

"We have to be a couple?" Lou coughed.

"Loouu, pleeease."

But Willow didn't need to beg. Lou would've done anything to make her friend feel better after the day she'd had. The fact that Lou had confusing feelings surrounding the man she was supposed to fake being in a relationship with was the only thing stopping her from jumping in.

"Willow, you've lived here longer than I have. If Noah and I pretend to be together, one of two things is going to happen. Either everyone will call us on it because they'll know it's not real, or everyone's going to think we're actually dating." Lou pinched the bridge of her nose.

Willow sighed. "Fine. I'll tell Bella you two aren't dating, but I'm thinking she's still going to want you both to come. Get here as soon as you can. We're at the bistro. Back table." The line cut off as Willow hung up.

Just as Lou was sliding Anne Mice off her lap, she got a text from Noah.

So ... you're getting dragged into this fake dating thing too?

A lightness filled Lou. She could practically hear his warm voice, and she could picture the way his grin would make dimples appear in his cheeks as he asked the question. Her reaction to his text reminded her that there was too much riding on her feelings for the man to pretend. She quickly typed a response.

I convinced Willow there's no way a small town like this is going to believe we're dating. Don't worry. We just have to show up as friends.

There was a longer pause than normal. Noah was usually so quick at texting back. Finally, he sent a reply.

Gotcha. See you there.

Did she detect a little relief in his words, or was it sadness? She knew there was a bit of disappointment buried deep inside her heart. Playing roles in a fake dating scheme sounded like a fun way to test out how it would feel. But the possible fun wasn't worth the emotional turmoil it might cause, not to mention the way it could complicate their friendship.

There was no time to contemplate those feelings. Willow needed her to hurry. Throwing on a floral-print summer dress, Lou finished the outfit with a light cardigan and some ballet flats. It was spring, but the nights still dropped lower than she was comfortable with facing without a jacket. She redid her bun so it was a little less wild and called it good.

The bistro was just one block up and over from the bookshop. Lou cut through the darkening alley. Normally, such a route wouldn't bother her, but the memory of that man lying faceup, eyes open in Willow's nursery, caused her to pick up her pace.

She spotted the group right away, mostly because they were seated at the largest table in the small space. Lou blinked as she took in Roy. She'd only ever seen him in dark suits, so it wasn't as if this charcoal-gray one should be a surprise, but somehow, he looked—dashing. His dark hair had been swept back and … was he wearing a pocket square? The woman sitting next to him had gorgeous long black hair. She wore tight dark blue jeans and a pink satin top. Easton was in a light-gray suit that Lou was pretty sure she'd seen him wear at work.

A hand landed on the small of Lou's back as someone came up behind her. She jumped to see Noah. He must've arrived just after her and had caught her surveying the group before she joined.

"What are we walking into here?" he whispered, leaning close.

His touch sent a shiver up Lou's back. It had been almost two years since Ben had died. Her parents had made it more than clear that she was allowed to move on anytime she felt ready. The thing was, she didn't know when that was.

Was it when she was attracted to someone else? That had been since the moment she'd met Noah, the day she'd moved to Button over a year ago. Or was she not ready until she stopped thinking of Ben every day? She doubted that day would come, or if she ever wanted it to.

As a former editor for a New York publishing house, Lou had lived and thrived in the comfort of rules. There were grammar rules and punctuation rules, and it had made her feel happy … safe. She wished there was some sort of rule book for moving on after you lost the love of your life. And even though Noah had been divorced for almost as long as Lou had been without Ben, she didn't know if he was ready to move on yet either.

Lou glanced up at Noah, trying to shove the indecisive thoughts aside and focus on her friend. "I can only imagine it's going to be terrible if they needed this much backup."

His lips pulled into a half smile that fell as his gaze landed on the table they were destined to join. "Bella?" He winced.

"You know her?" Lou asked, hoping for information about Roy's new mystery girlfriend.

Noah groaned. "Easton and I went to high school with her. She's … difficult." He ran a hand down his face.

Lou finally got a good look at what he was wearing. Being a vet, Noah was usually in scrubs, often covered by his long white jacket. If he wasn't working at his clinic, he was helping at his family's quilt shop, Material Girls. And even though he wore the standard pink apron when he was there, it was over his normal wardrobe of jeans or work pants and a button-up flannel shirt.

At that moment, however, Noah wore dark blue slacks, a light-blue button-up shirt, and a matching set of light-brown leather shoes and belt. The sleeves of his shirt were still rolled up to show his muscular forearms, but he was dressed fancier than Lou had seen him.

"You look nice," she said, realizing that she'd been ogling him a little and that she should probably say something to make it less awkward.

"Thank you." His grin reached his eyes as he took in her appearance. "As do you. Marigold would be obsessed with that dress. She informed me today that she's 'really into prints, Dad.'" He made his voice sound like a teenage girl and led Lou forward toward the table.

"Noooo, she's only ten. How is she growing up so fast?" Lou complained. Even though she had teenage nieces whom she loved, it was hard to see them shed their innocent childhood personas for the more grown-up teenage versions.

Noah clasped a hand to his chest as if his heart ached. "Tell me about it. I had this momentary overprotective-dad millisecond where I thought about locking her in her room so she would stop growing up. If only that worked."

They shared a laugh and then headed toward the table in the back of the restaurant, unsure what they were about to get involved in.

CHAPTER 5

Willow locked on to Lou and Noah as they approached. She stood, grabbing for their hands, and led them over to the remaining seats around the large table.

"Here they are. I'm so glad you could make it!" Willow's eye twitched as she practically shoved Lou into her seat. "Bella. Roy. These are our friends, Noah and Lou."

Roy glanced from Willow to Lou, then Noah. "Yeah, Willow. I know them. Lou and I just solved a case together a few months ago."

Lou's eyes widened at his admission. *She'd* considered their solution a joint venture, but didn't realize Roy would admit that she had anything to do with it. Maybe she had more of his respect than she thought.

Bella leaned forward. "I don't know Lou," she said in such an aggressive way that Lou felt the need to lean back.

"Louisa Henry," Lou said with a sheepish wave. "I own the bookshop around the corner."

"She's my best friend," Willow added, shooting Lou a grateful look.

Dark eyebrow rising as she took in Lou, Bella said, "Ah, the one with all the cats, who sells books?" she asked in disgust.

Lou nodded, though, based on Bella's tone, it sounded more like she was admitting to having boils and selling severed toes.

"Lou and Noah work together to find stray cats homes. She keeps them in the bookshop, so people who come in to shop can get to know the cats and spend time with them," Easton explained.

Bella glanced at him. "Sweet." The word was quick, like an obligation. She immediately turned to Noah. "No-ah, you didn't tell me you were dating again. I was so sad to hear when you and Cass broke up." She swatted at him across the table.

Noah messed with his napkin, his cheeks turning a light red.

"Oh, sorry for the confusion. Noah and I are here as friends," Lou jumped in, hoping to rescue the poor man.

He smiled through the grimace her comment provoked. "I haven't seen you in a while, Bella. What have you been up to lately?"

She sighed as if it was a chore to think about how to condense so much into a single sentence. "I'm set to take over the family company, and I'm getting my feet wet with all the day-to-day operations."

Lou wasn't upset when the server arrived to take their order and give them some more bread, effectively interrupting Bella before she could talk anymore about her family business.

They were in the middle of breaking apart and buttering slices of bread, except Bella because she *just didn't do carbs if she could help it*, when Bella said, "So, Willow. I can't believe what happened at your nursery today. What are you going to do?"

Both Willow and Roy gawked at her.

"Uh, babe, how'd you hear about that?" Roy asked, the words croaking out of a dry throat, proving he hadn't been the one to fill her in on the murder or any of the details.

She rolled her eyes. "I have connections, *babe*." The way she emphasized the word made Lou wonder if she was mad at him for questioning her or if she wasn't okay with his use of the nickname. "I also heard that the new Ryde driver ... Manny?" She squinted one eye as she looked up, unsure if that was correct.

"Martie," all five answered for her.

"Right. Martie. She found the dead guy's phone in her car." Bella widened her eyes for effect. "She picked up someone with the same name as the victim last night, but it was obviously the killer using the guy's phone."

Willow and Lou shared a quick look. That was news to them.

From the way Roy coughed and cut a glare at his girlfriend, it wasn't news to him. "Bella, seriously. Where did you hear that?"

She shot him a bored scowl back, as if she couldn't believe he might make her repeat her line about connections. Instead of answering Roy, Bella gawked at the others at the table. "Can you imagine that? Martie must've given the killer a ride away from the nursery after that guy was killed." She shivered.

Lou had so many questions.

"Wait. Could Martie describe the person?" Willow asked.

"Why do you want to know?" Roy cocked an eyebrow at her.

Willow flattened her expression. "Because that could help clear my name."

"No, Martie said they were all covered up, and the person didn't talk," Bella answered Willow's question. "It's kind of clever, don't you think? They ordered the getaway car using the dead guy's phone and Ryde account so it couldn't be traced back to them. And they had Martie drop them off at that big shopping center, The Trails, in Kirk."

Roy was clenching his jaw so tight Lou was afraid he might break a tooth. "That's *really* enough, Bella."

Bella rolled her eyes and then turned her attention back to Willow. "But seriously, all of this happened at the same time you were supposed to open *and* that you lost your goat?"

Willow's shoulders sank forward as if the reminder of her worries sat on them like a physical weight.

"We'll find Steve," Easton said, jumping in to help Willow. "And Roy will figure out what happened at the nursery last night. I have complete faith in his ability as a detective." The hard tone Easton adopted as he gave Roy the compliment made it sound a little more threatening than Easton probably realized, as if he were letting him know that if he didn't, there would be problems.

"I hope so." Willow gave Easton, and then Roy, a small smile.

Easton wrapped an arm around Willow's shoulders and pulled her into a side hug, kissing the top of her head.

"But what will you do? This nursery was your dream," Bella said, surprising Lou with the amount of concern the woman was suddenly showing for Willow. Maybe they'd gotten off on the wrong foot.

Willow nodded. "This week was going to be a soft opening for locals. I didn't set the opening day until next Friday for any of the flyers I put out in the rest of the county."

"Look at you. So smart. Easton, you picked a smart one here." Bella grinned insincerely.

Easton lifted his chin with pride. "I definitely did." He placed his hand over Willow's on the table.

Their food arrived, bringing a much-needed change to the conversation. For a while, it moved into how Easton, Noah, and Bella had all known each other since high school, when Bella's family moved to town. Then Bella drilled Lou with questions about what it was like living in New York City.

"And you just picked up your whole life and moved across the country?" Bella asked Lou, her intense eye contact making Lou a little nervous as she attempted to eat her dinner.

Lou coughed, holding the back of her hand up to cover

her mouth. Her cheeks reddened at the reality behind the answer to that question.

This time, it was Willow who jumped in to rescue Lou. "She lost her husband."

"Lost? Like Willow's goat?" Bella joked, but her smile fell as she was met with blank, upset stares from the other side of the table. "Omigosh, like *lost*." Her cheeks turned red. "I'm so sorry. I didn't mean to make light of that."

Lou waved her fork in the air. "It's okay."

"It's not." Bella stood and rounded the table, pulling Lou into a bone-crushing hug. Once she was seated again, she said, "Sorry for your loss. Is what happened at Willow's today a complete kick in the gut for you?"

Swallowing, Lou shook her head. "I've seen other bodies before. I'm okay."

Bella clicked her tongue. "Right. New York City."

Lou and Noah shared a private grin, knowing most of them had happened here in the small town of Button.

Bella asked, "So if you didn't do it, Willow, who do you think did?"

Roy coughed. "Babe."

Bella sent him a glare that told him not to try her, before turning her attention back to Willow.

Willow's eyes closed out of fatigue. It had been a long day. "I honestly don't know. That's the scary part. I mean, the guy was an auditor for the Department of Agriculture. It's pretty hard to think of him making anyone mad enough to kill him. It's just plants."

"You never know." Bella arched an eyebrow. "Plants are worth money like everything else. And once you get enough of it involved, anything can become something worth killing over."

Lou surprised herself by agreeing with Bella for once that evening. "That's true," she said in sudden thought. "And if the guy was threatening to fine and prevent Willow from opening over some disease that most likely wasn't even present in her plants, maybe he threatened to shut down someone else too."

Bella nodded. "See? You're getting it." She tapped Roy's shoulder. "Roy here says there needs to be more than just money at stake to kill someone, but he forgets that with money also comes love and obsession." She glanced up just as the server came over with dessert menus.

Roy folded his napkin and placed it on the table. "Okay, everyone. That's enough. Babe, you don't need to talk anymore about the case." Turning his scowl toward Lou and Willow, he added, "And if I hear about either of you trying to figure this out on your own, I will take it as an admission that you really are guilty of what happened to that man last night."

"How would trying to solve it show you Willow's guilty?" Lou spat out the question, surprising herself with the level of anger and frustration backing her words.

Roy glared at her. "Because she'd obviously be trying to point the finger elsewhere. That's what guilty people do. They distract."

"Like I was guilty of the murder last fall?" Lou narrowed her eyes at Roy. "You were so sure it was me, and you turned out to be wrong then. Just like you're wrong now."

"You can tell she's from New York," Bella muttered under her breath.

"I need you to calm down." Roy held up a hand toward Lou.

The gesture only made her see more red. "I'll calm down when you look for the actual killer instead of focusing on the innocent person who is a secondary victim in this crime. Think about it, *Roy*," she said, his name curling around her tongue like an insult. "Why would Willow postpone the grand opening of her business, her life's dream? Why would she put any of that at risk?"

"Exactly, it's her dream," he cut back. "So, if that auditor was going to stand in the way, she might've done anything to clear the path."

Lou stood, fishing out money from her wallet and dropping it on the table. "I'm sorry," she said to Willow. "I can't sit here with him anymore."

With that, she left the restaurant, painfully aware of the fact that every eye was on her as she pushed through the door.

CHAPTER 6

Lou had stomped halfway down the block before she heard her name being called behind her. She stopped, glancing over her shoulder to see Noah jogging her way. The angry scowl her face had been pulled into softened at the sight of him.

"That was something," he said, shoving his hands into his pockets as he fell in step with her.

"Sorry." She cringed.

Noah chuckled. "Never apologize to me for putting that guy in his place." He ran a hand through his hair. "And now that he's with Bella, it's almost as if they're high-lighting all the worst parts of each other. She has fewer boundaries than ever before, and any sense of humility he had has been replaced by this bravado trying to impress her."

Lou trained her eyes on her hands. "Still, I shouldn't have blown up like that. It's never helpful, especially after the day Willow's had." She slowed, sending a regretful glance at the bistro, as she wondered whether she should go back and apologize.

As if she knew she was thinking about her, Willow texted at that moment. Lou pulled out her phone.

> That was amazing. You're my hero forever.
> Thank you for standing up for me.

Lou held up a finger to Noah. "It's Willow. Sorry, I'm going to reply."

He came to a stop alongside her as she typed.

> Oh, phew. I was worried I went overboard.
> Sorry. Roy just grates on my nerves, and
> Bella took away my last ounce of patience.
> Want me to come back?

> No. You're good. We're ordering desserts
> to go. Roy and Bella left too.

> Let me know if you need anything tonight.
> Love you.

> Love you too. Easton and I are going to
> watch a movie with my parents while we
> eat all these desserts and try to forget that
> today ever happened. I'll stop by the
> bookshop in the morning.

Lou hoped the movie with Willow's parents went better than the dinner just had. Honestly, between Joel and Easton, it had the possibility of ending with just as much hostility.

"Willow's good," she informed Noah as she tucked her

phone back into her purse.

He adjusted the collar on his button-up shirt. "I can't believe how well she's doing, considering everything."

"As strong as she is, I think she might still be in shock, to be honest." Lou started walking toward Thread Lane. "I doubt everything has settled in her mind yet. And her worries are constantly bouncing back and forth between the nursery and Steve."

They stopped at the corner of Thread Lane and Stitch Street.

"That makes sense. Well, I'm glad she'll have you and Easton to help her when it does finally hit. That's going to be a lot to process." His gaze flicked down the street. "Since we didn't get dessert, what do you say to some ice cream?"

Scoop O' Button was more than just Lou's neighboring business. They were also the home of the best ice cream Lou had ever tasted. And even though she was tempted by their seasonal flavors all year round, it became almost impossible to say no once the weather warmed up.

"I'd say, absolutely." Lou followed him down the street.

Walking inside was like stepping foot into a cloud of cotton candy. The whole place smelled like sweet cream, spun sugar, and toasted waffle cones. Ribs Randall smiled a gap-toothed grin at them from behind the counter. No one was sure what his actual name was, but he insisted everyone call him Ribs because that's what his army pals called him, so it was the only name that mattered.

Hillary, the owner of the ice cream shop, exclusively hired war veterans. Her father had been one before he'd passed, just before she'd opened Scoop, and she wanted to keep his memory alive, not to mention hoping to give the veterans a sweet job to contrast all the sour they'd experienced already in their lives.

"Evening, neighbor," Ribs called out in his gravelly voice. "And doc." He inclined his head toward them at the same time as he snapped a fresh pair of gloves onto his hands. "What can I do for you tonight?"

Lou's eyes pored over the handwritten list of flavors, landing on her favorites. She adored the local marionberry, couldn't go a month without getting the coffee cream, and loved the cotton candy because it made her feel like a kid all over again. But tonight, something new caught her attention.

"What's a s'mores sundae?" Lou could feel her mouth water just thinking about the possibilities.

Ribs adopted a similarly awestruck look. "Ahhh, a recent addition. Hillary made a s'mores ice cream last week. It's got a marshmallow base with chocolate and graham cracker chunks. But the sundae means we do a layer of marshmallow fluff, two scoops of the s'mores ice cream, cover it in hot fudge, jab some graham crackers in it, and then toast two homemade marshmallows on the top." His expression danced with excitement. "She's been making the marshmallows here, by hand. They're better than anything you've tasted."

Lou and Noah shared a look, nodding at each other and then at Ribs.

"I think we have to get one of those," Noah said. "Do you mind splitting? I probably *could* eat one all by myself, but I don't know if I *should*."

Lou laughed. "Splitting one sounds perfect."

"And can I get a pint of the cotton candy to go?" Noah added. "Marigold will be very cross with me if she finds out I came without her," he explained.

"Makes sense." Lou beamed.

Ribs worked on their sundae, but he kept shooting wary glances over at Lou while he scooped and layered. At first, Lou wondered if he found it odd to see Lou and Noah there together. Did he think they were on a date? They were friends and hung out together all the time. What about tonight made it feel different? Maybe their fancier clothing was giving the locals pause. Lou realized that getting ice cream, just the two of them, while wearing clothes that looked like they were on a date was probably just as dangerous as if they had pretended to be a couple for the dinner that night. Was the local gossip mill already churning? Or would Ribs start it after they left?

As it turned out, Lou didn't need to worry. The truth behind Ribs's concerned stares came to light as he used a small butane torch to toast the fluffy marshmallows on top.

"How's Miss Willow doing today?" Ribs asked, the light of the flame reflecting in his dark eyes as he watched the marshmallows brown.

Lou relaxed. It wasn't about her and Noah at all, just genuine concern for Willow. Lou flinched as she said, "Not great. She's pretty worried."

"I'd bet. I'd bet." Ribs repeated the line slower the second time. He checked left and then right before leaning close to Lou. "You didn't hear it from me, but my buddy in Brine heard someone having a heckuva fight with that same

Bramble fella last week. Our Willow's not alone, by a long shot."

Lou shot a quick glance over at Noah. "Did your friend tell you who that person was?" she asked Ribs as conversationally as she could.

Ribs dipped his head as he handed the sundae across the counter to Noah. "He's having his front yard landscaped. Some guy with the last name Pine."

"Pine from Brine," Noah mused, cradling the dessert as if it were precious cargo.

Ribs clapped his hands together. "I'll get that pint going for you while the two of you eat."

Noah grabbed two spoons and led Lou over to one of the tables. They sat across from each other as they each dug their spoon into opposite ends of the sundae. Lou's spoon cut through the crunchy exterior of the toasted marshmallow before sinking through the hot fudge and scooping into the ice cream. She waited for Noah as they took their first bites together.

"That's the greatest thing I've ever tasted." Lou was pretty sure her eyes crossed in delight.

Noah licked his spoon clean. "I think you're right." He took another bite, but his eyes narrowed as he watched her.

"What?" She laughed, running her fingers around her lips to make sure she didn't have any chocolate sauce or sticky marshmallow on her face.

"Are you thinking what I'm thinking?" Noah asked with a sly smile.

Lou almost melted, just like the fudge on their sundae, at the deepness of Noah's voice and the way his mischievous eyes danced with an idea. She didn't know what *he* was thinking, but her thoughts were of the somewhat more dangerous, friendship-line-crossing kind, so she waited to see what he said.

"A man in the town over had a fight with the man who showed up dead in Willow's nursery today." Noah's eyebrows rose with interest. "He seems worth looking into."

Lou blinked. Right. She'd been hit with the same realization just a moment before. The delicious ice cream and long day had obviously messed with her ability to be rational.

"Yes, just what I was thinking too," she said, sure it was easier to lean into the lie than admit she'd been thinking of herself—specifically her and Noah—rather than focusing on her friend who was in trouble.

Lou reluctantly set down her spoon and brought out her phone. She searched for Pine Landscaping Brine, WA, and hit enter. A few hits came up, but they all seemed to be for the same company, one run by none other than Jeremiah Pine.

"I think this is our guy." Lou turned the phone so it faced Noah. "I think he's the one Ribs said his friend heard fighting with the auditor."

"A landscaper. That makes sense. And Brine is in Lakeside County, so he'd be under the same jurisdiction as Willow." Noah took another bite and studied Lou. "What are you going to do?"

Lou swallowed, shutting off her phone and placing it on the table. "Roy told us not to get involved, in no uncertain terms." She took another delectable bite of the s'mores sundae.

Noah watched her again in that unnerving way. "Yeah, I heard that. Are you going to listen to him?"

Licking her spoon, Lou said, "I haven't decided yet."

THE NEXT MORNING, Lou showed up at Willow's house before the bookshop was supposed to open, with coffees and desserts in hand. She'd placed a sign on the bookshop door that announced another full-day closure and an apology for the inconvenience. It would really only be a surprise to nonlocals. Anyone from Button would assume Lou would need to be with Willow, supporting her in such a dark time.

And while Lou had her own key, she stood at the front door and knocked, just in case Willow wasn't expecting her best friend that morning. The moment she knocked, however, her phone buzzed with a text.

Out back. On the deck. Come on through.

It was from Willow. She must've heard Lou banging on the door.

Balancing the travel tray of coffees and the various flaky pastries, she dug out her key and opened the door. Lou walked through the house, making her way through the living room and out onto the deck. Willow was sitting on the patio, staring out at OC and the field beyond the paddocks.

And even though Willow had a mug with the last few tablespoons of her first cup of coffee in the bottom, Lou swapped the mug with the to-go cup she'd brought. She placed a croissant in Willow's other hand. Job done, she had a seat and pulled her own breakfast from the bag.

"Your parents still sleeping?" Lou glanced back at the house.

Ramona and Joel were staying in Willow's spare bedroom, something Lou knew to be both a blessing and a curse. While both women enjoyed having their parents visit, it was tough living with someone who had once made the household rules, only to have the roles reversed.

Willow cocked an eyebrow. "They headed home this morning, actually."

"What?" Lou coughed out the word. "Did your dad and Easton get in a fight last night during the movie?"

"Fight? No." Willow snorted. "Though they shot each other dirty looks the whole time and made sure they had opposite opinions about *everything*."

"And that's why they left?" Lou asked, slightly disappointed in Ramona and Joel for leaving their daughter during such a tough time.

Willow shook her head. "They were supposed to leave tonight anyway, but Mom had a work emergency and had to go back a little early." Willow shrugged, showing she was okay with the change in plans. "But enough about Mom and Dad. I want to hear about what happened once Noah ran after you yesterday." She waggled her eyebrows.

Lou pressed her lips together. She wasn't sure what to say. And even though she and Willow had been friends forever, and they told each other everything, Lou didn't know exactly how to put what she was feeling into words. "We got a lead in the Harley Bramble case, actually." She winced and sipped on her latte, hoping Willow wouldn't get too mad that she'd been thinking about doing some investigating behind Roy's back.

Willow set down her latte. "Thank goodness. I do not trust Roy to sort this out."

Lou laughed in relief. "Roy's not a bad detective, but he is stubborn, and I can see him looking for evidence that proves his first theory correct."

"Yeah. And you're looking at his first theory." Willow hunched her shoulders in defeat.

Lou gave Willow a pointed look. "Last night, Ribs was telling me that his buddy in Brine had heard someone fighting with Harley Bramble last week."

"Ribs?" Willow folded her arms in front of herself in a pout. "You got ice cream?"

"You ate three desserts from the bistro." Lou rolled her eyes at her friend.

"Touché." Willow bent her head forward in concession. "Okay, so I wasn't the only one who fought with the auditor."

"You weren't the only one with motive to want him dead," Lou clarified. She held a hand up. "Not saying you wanted him dead, it's just—"

Willow nodded. "I know what you meant." Her expression fell. "And you said the person's in Brine?"

The town to the east of Button was infamous for its pickle-themed streets and the sour disposition of its inhabitants. Lou worried Willow would be reluctant to visit.

Instead, she said, "That tracks. If there are killers around here, I'd bet it's one of them."

That was harsh, even for Willow. Her friend was under a lot of stress, though, so she let it slide. "What do you say to going and checking out this landscaper with me?"

"Sure," Willow scoffed. "It's not like I have anything better to do."

Sadness crowded the outdoor furniture, adding to the to-go cups of coffee and pastry bags. Willow was supposed to be in the full swing of her opening week, giddy with the feeling of a dream come true and excited for the possibilities to come. She'd also combed the entire town for Steve. If he was out there, he wasn't somewhere they were going to find by driving or walking along the roads.

"A little road trip next door will be good to take your mind off everything," Lou said.

At that moment, movement in the field caught Lou's eye. Willow saw it, too, by the way she sat up straight and squinted past OC's paddock. A small gray animal picked its way through the tall grass toward Willow's house.

Willow inhaled sharply. "Steve?"

CHAPTER 7

Abandoning their coffees, Lou and Willow raced through the garden, stopping at the gate to the field, next to the paddocks. Willow climbed onto the gate, shielding her eyes from the morning sunshine as she peered out at the animal.

OC trotted over to the end of the paddock. He followed their gazes and watched the field as well. The moment he caught sight of the small animal moving in the grass, his nostrils flared and he arched his muscular neck. Lou wanted to laugh. For a giant beast, weighing over a thousand pounds, OC got so scared of … well, everything.

But the fact that he would've recognized his friend wasn't lost on Lou or Willow.

"It's a little small to be Steve, don't you think?" Willow's question was quiet but filled to the brim with emotions, namely sadness.

Lou stepped up to the gate, peering through the metal slats. She had to admit that Willow had a point. It was a little short to be Steve. But as her excitement waned, Lou's curiosity intensified.

If the creature wasn't the missing pygmy goat, what was it?

As if it knew they needed some kind of solid answer, the thing chose that moment to hitch a thin gray tail high in the air as it picked its way through the grass. The very tip of the gray tail was white.

"A cat?" Lou breathed out the question.

"I've never seen a cat around here before," Willow said, climbing down off the gate so she could unlatch it and pull it toward her.

Lou, who felt as if she saw cats wherever she went, wasn't surprised. Ever since she'd dedicated her bookshop to be a rescue cat sanctuary, cats just seemed to fall into her lap. Most of the time, however, they had come to Lou through Noah or because an owner had left them on Lou's front doorstep or in her back alley. A cat had never found her out and about in the wild since her very first foster, an orange kitten named Romeow.

Two little gray ears poked up over the grass as it trotted toward the women. It let out a cute, high-pitched meow. It wasn't a meow of terror or even of longing, like Lou expected from a feline making such a point to walk directly toward two humans. The meow was conversational, akin to a "Good morning. How are you today?" from a friendly neighbor.

As the cat drew closer, Lou could see that the splotch of white on the end of its tail wasn't the only white on its body. A couple of its feet were socked in white, visible as it lifted paw after paw delicately through the grass. It also had a white spot over one eye in an adorable patch.

"Good morning to you too," Lou greeted it, feeling that was the most proper way to respond to the greeting the gray cat had given them.

It trotted the last few feet, coming out of the taller grass. Instead of stopping to check them out, the cat showed no hesitation as it strode over and rubbed up against their shins, repeating its meowed salutation.

"Well, aren't you just the cutest thing?" Lou bent to pet the cat.

Willow pushed aside her disappointment at it not being Steve and knelt, calling the animal over to her. It abandoned Lou and walked over to Willow, reaching up to headbutt her hand. In the same movement, it rolled its body in midair and flopped onto its side. The women laughed. OC snorted, eyeing the creature from his paddock as if it might jump at him in attack at any moment.

"It sure is friendly," Lou said as the cat squirmed on the ground, pieces of dried grass and hay sticking to its beautiful, bluish-gray fur.

"And it doesn't have a collar." Willow stood, shielding her eyes once more as she surveyed the houses closest to her. "He's not Easton's," she narrated as she turned in a circle. "And the Jamesons can't have any pets because of their rental agreement," she said, motioning to the small house perched through the trees on the edge of her property, in the direction the cat had come from. "I mean, he could've come from the Forest Pond neighborhood, along Pin Street, but that's pretty far."

"I guess this means we need to chat with Noah." Lou stood, remembering that her phone was still in her purse back on the deck with their breakfast.

Willow turned back too. The gray cat rolled to its feet and trotted after the women as they walked toward Willow's house, like it was one of them. Checking the time, Lou realized Noah might already be seeing patients. She texted him first.

> Hey, found a stray at Willow's today. Any chance I can bring it by this morning? No rush on the exam, I just don't want to bring him to the bookstore until we know if he's healthy or who he belongs to.

She waited a few seconds, smiling as the cat jumped into one of the chairs around the table and sat, as if it were just another human. And even though the creature had brought some much-needed levity to their morning, it didn't change the fact that Willow and Lou had errands to run in Brine. Well, errands was a pretty soft way to describe figuring out who'd really killed Harley Bramble.

Feeling the pressure to get moving, Lou said, "I should just call Kathleen. We can drop him off with her, and she can fill in Noah once he has a break in appointments."

Kathleen was the office manager for the Button Veterinary Clinic. The shrewd woman was both whip-smart and efficient, and she had a huge heart for animals. But before Lou could even dial the number, she received a response from Noah.

Sure! Bring it by. I've got some time later in my schedule. I can check if it's microchipped and give it an exam.

"Oh, perfect. He says to bring it by," Lou explained. "We can drop it by the clinic on our way out of town."

At the reminder of where they were headed, Willow groaned and downed a large gulp of her latte, as if she would need the caffeine. "Great." She gave Lou a wan smile. "Let's hurry."

Lou brushed off the flatness in her tone. "Now we just have to figure out how to get you into the car." She studied the cat. While she had many cat crates back at the bookshop, she didn't have any in her car. "I think I need to start traveling with at least one crate," she said.

"Probably," Willow said. "Especially since it seems cats are now seeking you out." She chuckled. "You're like some kind of cat-specific cartoon princess."

"I wish. Do you have an empty cardboard box I could use?" Lou used her hands to mime the approximate size and shape she thought might work.

"In the garage." Willow led the way inside.

Unsurprisingly, the cat followed, skirting inside the house right along with them.

"Maybe I don't even need the box." Lou examined the cat as it stopped at their feet. "This thing is more like a dog than a cat."

Opening the garage, Willow walked over to a shelf and plucked an empty cardboard box from a pile she had yet to break down. Trying out a hunch, Lou put it on the ground and waited. The cat immediately jumped into the box.

Lou grinned. "That was easy."

She picked up the box, cat and all, and Willow opened the garage so they could leave through there. Once they were in Lou's car—Lou folded down the back seats in her hatchback so they could see the cat—it jumped out of the box to roam around the trunk area. That was okay. She had a feeling it wouldn't be too difficult to get him back inside once they stopped at the clinic.

"Ah, Noah told me we were expecting a new friend this morning," Kathleen said, standing as Lou and Willow entered, carrying the new cat in the box.

Lou hadn't even needed to close the flaps on the top. The cat was so content being with them. The realization made her a little worried that it might be sad to be left behind, but it turned out that the cat just generally enjoyed being around people. It didn't really matter which people.

Once they handed the box over to Kathleen so she could take him back to a holding crate, he turned his adoring stare from Lou and Willow to Kathleen.

"We'll be running errands for a bit, but I'll be back later to pick him up," Lou said, adding, "or return him to his people, depending on what Noah finds." It was always a possibility that the cat was microchipped and that it would be as simple as reuniting it with its family.

Kathleen waved goodbye, allowing Willow and Lou to head to their destination. Willow's shoulders held a new tension as they climbed back into Lou's car, but Lou brushed it off. Willow, like many other Button residents, found Brine to be not only tacky but somewhat threatening. Not competitively, but like they worried the town to the east might rub off on them or ruin their chances of attracting tourists. It was almost as if Brine was a dilapidated home in a neighborhood, bringing down the value of every other house around it.

As much as Lou fit in right away in Button, immediately feeling like one of the locals who'd been there their whole lives, her feelings on Brine were the one area she differed from the other locals. She found the smaller town's quirkiness charming. If they hadn't been going to question someone in a murder investigation, she would've been more excited, of course, but any chance to visit the funky town felt like an adventure to Lou.

"Okay, we're looking for a landscaper, right?" Willow asked as they hit the road, pulling up her maps app so they would have directions.

"His last name is Pine," Lou confirmed.

Willow poked at her screen for a few moments before saying, "Pine Landscaping, in Brine, Washington. That's probably it. Jeremiah Pine?"

"That's him." Lou gripped the steering wheel a little tighter as she took a turn through downtown.

"And you think it's smart for us to go directly to him and ask him about Harley, if he might be the killer?" Willow swallowed as her finger hovered over the screen, not yet ready to commit to his farm as their destination.

Lou contemplated that. "Hmmm, you're right. That might not be the smartest course of action." It was then that their conversation with Roy last night came to mind. "Do you think we should abandon the idea of doing this ourselves and tell Roy? He said that we'd both be in hot water if he caught us trying to investigate."

Willow nodded somberly, as if she replayed that conversation in her mind.

"What if we did a little asking around in town first? Just to be safe." Lou suggested.

"That sounds smart." Willow dropped her phone into her lap. "In that case, I don't need directions to get you to Brine. Just drive toward the scent of pickles." She chuckled to herself.

"Get all your pickle jokes out now," Lou warned her. "Making fun of them won't help us get the answers we need."

Willow mimed locking her lips tight and throwing away the key. "Yes, ma'am." They sat in silence for a beat until Willow took the imaginary key and unlocked her mouth, saying, "It's just that the jokes write themselves, so I'm in a *pickle* about what to do. Really, Lou. It's quite the *dill-emma*. It's not like I *relish* making fun of their town."

"That last one was particularly sour." Lou cackled as she drove toward the pickle-themed town.

CHAPTER 8

Lou wasn't sure where the best place to gather intel was in the neighboring town, but she knew that the place with the most gossip in Button was usually the local coffeehouse. And even if it wasn't the hub of local information, they would at least be able to hang out for a while under the guise of drinking coffee and chatting.

She just hoped they wouldn't become jittery after so much caffeine. Willing to take that risk, she parked in one of the few spots in front of the Briny Bean.

Just as with the last time she'd entered, hundreds of pickle ornaments hung from the ceiling. Even though they were the kind one might find on a Christmas tree, it appeared that the ornaments stayed up all year round.

Lou and Willow immediately seemed out of place as all eyes turned to them. It was late morning, so it probably wasn't even peak hours for the coffeehouse, but the place was packed. From the stares they got, Lou felt confident guessing the patrons filling almost every seat were locals. Which highlighted yet another difference between Button and Brine. People in Button turned to look at newcomers with smiles on their faces in a way that welcomed guests, encouraging them to stay awhile and to return once they left. The people of Brine made visitors feel as though they were doing everything wrong, that they shouldn't even be there.

Their intense stares even made Lou question whether she knew the correct way to order coffee or if this town did it differently and she really was messing it up.

"Okay, I think I'm seeing your point of view a little more clearly now," Lou whispered to Willow as they stepped aside after having paid for their coffees.

They'd come last summer, when Lou's nieces had visited. But the teenagers were wildly friendly and outgoing, and Lou had been so entertained by their enjoyment of the pickle town that she hadn't noticed the intense disdain roiling off almost every local in the joint.

"I told you so," Willow said through clenched teeth, moving her lips as little as possible.

"It's definitely going to make finding information about this Jeremiah guy harder." Lou scanned the place. The people didn't even look away, not worried at all about being caught staring.

Willow nodded. "Tell me about it. This pickle jar's lid is screwed on tight." She bit back a giggle.

Lou smacked her playfully. They took their coffees when the disinterested barista handed them over, and they settled into the only two seats left, at a table that seemed more like an afterthought at the mouth of the hallway to the bathroom. A corkboard crowded with flyers, took up the wall space next to them. A paper with tabs meant to be ripped off, fluttered in Willow's face as someone walked past them on the way to the bathroom. Lou drummed her fingers on the table as she thought.

Willow swatted the paper away as she sipped at her coffee in a disgruntled hunch. Lou's eye was drawn to the overcrowded corkboard. On it, she recognized the name of the psychic they'd gone to see last summer. Francine had been instrumental in helping them crack the mystery they'd been trying to solve. Maybe she could help them again.

And, if she's booked up, there are two other psychics in town, Lou thought to herself.

But then something else on the bulletin board caught Lou's attention. A smile curved over her lips. Maybe they wouldn't need a psychic after all.

"What are you smiling about?" Willow asked with an added grumble of unease.

Lou focused on the board next to Willow. "Are you seeing what I'm seeing?"

Willow was not. She huffed and cut her gaze to the side so she could reluctantly peruse the random business cards, offers for tutoring, and announcements about local events—many long since passed.

"You're interested in having Josh make a clay figurine of your pet's likeness?" Willow guessed with a playful smirk.

Lou motioned beyond that flyer, toward the one next to Willow's ear. "That one, for mulch."

Willow cocked her head. "You want to buy some mulch from Marisol? Lou, you don't even have a yard."

It was true. The most landscaping Lou could do was fiddle with the indoor plants she'd accumulated over the past year and tend to the large potted plants Willow liked to set on either side of the entrance to the bookshop. They changed with the season and depended on what Willow was trying to find a place for at that moment. Right now, two beautiful forsythia shrubs were lighting up the entrance to Whiskers and Words with their bright yellow blooms. Lou loved catching the moment when customers or passersby caught sight of the cheerful plants and their vibrant flowers; it usually put a huge smile on their faces.

Lou laughed. "No, I don't need any mulch, but look at the bottom, where it explains how to get hold of Marisol."

"At the garden center?" Willow frowned.

"Yes. I think Marisol might be a good person to talk to," Lou explained. "Not only does she *have more mulch than she knows what to do with*, but she might have a specifically close relationship with a local landscaper if she works at a business he likely frequents."

Understanding washed over Willow. "Oh, right. Yeah, that makes sense."

"And if she won't talk, we can at least check in with Francine." Lou gestured to the psychic's card tacked to the board in the upper left-hand corner, mostly covering a flyer for the large Northwest Plants tulip farm up north.

Willow's eyes went wide. "I forgot about Francine. Are you sure we shouldn't just go straight there?"

Lou wanted to see where the garden center lead went first. "Let's give Marisol a shot."

"Okay." Willow took another sip of her coffee and stood, leaning down to whisper, "We'd better leave now, then, because my coffee's going to get cold in this frosty environment if we stay much longer."

The two of them skirted out of the café. Contained in the same block as the Briney Bean was a bakery and a pizza restaurant. The Salty Slice was housed in a triangle-shaped building.

"Ha, a pizza place in the shape of a slice. That's good." Lou chuckled to herself as she followed Willow down the block.

Willow shot her an exasperated scowl. At the end of the block, she stopped to cross Gherkin Street. But they didn't walk straight across, mostly because there were no buildings there. A minor road called Half-Sour Street cut through the next block, creating two floating triangles of space. The auto-repair shop to the left and the garden center to their right were both housed in triangular buildings.

"These picklers really like triangles," Lou muttered to herself as they veered right toward the garden and hardware center.

From the hunch of Willow's shoulders, Lou could tell her friend wasn't crazy about asking for help. Her attitude only worsened as she eyed a sad display of spring plants in front of the store. They were small, with leaves that looked a little wilted and discolored. She shot Lou a glare as if the poor stock proved they shouldn't come there for help.

The automatic doors squealed as they opened, enveloping Lou and Willow in the familiar scent of fertilizer and soil. The checkout area had one long counter where two registers sat, one on each end. Although there were two computers, only one woman stood behind the counter. She smiled a greeting and welcomed Lou and Willow into the store.

"That might be Marisol. We should go talk to her," Lou whispered out of the side of her mouth.

But when she turned to see if Willow was in agreement, she was gone.

"Willow?" Lou continued to whisper for some unknown reason. She spun around, just in time to catch the last wisps of brown hair of Willow's ponytail whip down an aisle. She darted after.

When she turned the corner, Lou found Willow clutching a garden hose, her eyes poring over the rest of the selection. She turned her intense stare toward Lou as she approached.

"They have that flexible fabric hose I've been searching for." Willow held it tighter to her body as if Lou might try to steal the thing. Her gaze cut back to the wall of hoses, and she gasped. "And the neat coiled one I was considering. It springs back like a slinky." She held it out toward Lou.

Laughing, Lou said, "Seems like you should've made a trip over here a lot sooner, then." Even though she'd seen the *rougher skin of the pickle,* so to speak, Lou maintained Willow was still taking her dislike of their neighboring town too far.

"Do you think we have time for me to shop around a little more?" Willow's eyes danced with possibilities.

Lou kicked at a small rock someone had tracked inside. "Sure. Plus, if you make purchases, that'll give us an excuse to talk to the woman I hope is named Marisol that works the register."

From there, a fifteen-minute buying spree commenced. Willow squealed in delight, and even giggled a few times, as she found some things she'd had on her garden wish list.

"Whoever does their purchasing is a genius. They've got all the best brands in stock. They definitely know their stuff." Willow stood over her haul like a dragon surveying its treasure.

"See?" Lou nudged her with an elbow as they turned the cart toward the checkout counter. "Branching out and getting over your prejudices is good."

Willow sighed. "Okay. Fine. You were right."

Lou beamed, turning her smile toward the woman behind the register as she waved them over.

"Looks like you're buying the entire store." The woman snorted out a delighted giggle, her brown curls bouncing as her shoulders shook with laughter. She was a good ten, maybe twenty years older than Lou and Willow, with rosy cheeks and wispy hair. "I don't even think I need to ask if you found everything you were searching for, like I normally do." Unfortunately, she wasn't wearing a name tag, so Lou still couldn't tell if she was the person they were hoping to meet.

Willow began loading the items onto the long, empty

counter so the woman could scan them. "It's a testament to whoever does your ordering. They deserve a raise."

The woman giggled again. "Well, since Marisol owns the place, I don't think she can give herself a raise, but I'm sure she'll be happy to hear the compliment."

At the name, Willow and Lou exchanged a knowing glance. If the woman was the business owner, she was even more likely to know the landscaper in question.

"Is Marisol around?" Lou asked. "We saw her flyer about mulch and were wondering if we could talk to her."

The woman narrowed her eyes. "She doesn't deliver outside of town limits."

"Oh, we don't actually want the mulch," Lou clarified. "We're hoping to ask her about a local landscaper. In fact, you might know him too. Jeremiah Pine?"

"Jeremiah?" The woman practically shivered with disgust. "Oh, sure. I know him." She muttered something about wishing she didn't. "You looking for some land-scaping help?"

Lou wasn't sure what it was about the woman, but she trusted her. "Actually, we heard he got into a fight with a man my friend here just found dead in her nursery the day she was supposed to open. We're trying to figure out if Jere-miah might have any information for us about that man and who might've wanted him dead."

The woman grumbled, "Getting in arguments? Sounds like the snake." That time, her aside was much clearer. It sounded like this woman had a big problem with Jeremiah.

"You're from that new Valley Nursery, aren't you?" A steely voice cut through the air.

Willow flinched as it hit her back. "I am. What's it to you?"

Lou felt like she was in the shoot-out scene of an old western movie as she turned around to find a woman about the same age as the one behind the register, standing with garden glove-clad hands on her hips at the edge of the charcoal display.

CHAPTER 9

Willow mirrored the woman's stance, placing her hands on her hips as well.

"Sydney, you haven't collected any payment yet, have you?" The woman peeled her glare from Willow for a split second while she checked with the woman behind the counter.

"We were just about to get to that, *Marisol*." Sydney emphasized the woman's name and widened her eyes at Lou and Willow as if trying to let them know they were dealing with the boss.

That had been clear to Lou since she'd laid eyes on the woman. But it wasn't the confidence or superiority that had done it. Lou recognized the same pride of ownership in this woman that she felt about Whiskers and Words and had seen in Willow over the last few months as the nursery had come together.

Marisol walked forward. "What do you want with Jeremiah?"

"Never mind, Lou. We should go. I shouldn't be surprised that this town would protect someone they despise." Willow glanced toward the door but didn't move. "I thought I needed all of this, but I should've known better than to buy anything from a garden store that sells plants as sad as the ones out front."

At that, instead of fuming like Lou expected her to, Marisol's shoulders slumped forward. "They're awful. I know." She shook her head. "But ever since the local places have gone out of business, a big corporation is the only supplier left, and they sell those lifeless excuses for plants."

"What about Jeremiah?" Lou asked. "It sounds like his landscaping business is going well. Where does he source his plants?"

"Pine Farm," Sydney said, in an *of course* kinda tone. "They're gorgeous." She turned red as she looked up at Marisol.

Lou didn't understand the problem. "Can't you carry stock from his farm?"

Sydney clicked her tongue, muttering something about trouble.

"He's my ex-husband, and the farm I used to live on is where he grows everything. Believe me when I say I don't want to get myself entangled in that place again." Marisol placed a hand on her hip.

Lou and Willow blinked, sharing a furtive glance. It seemed that Lou had been more correct than she'd realized when she guessed Marisol would be a good person to ask about Jeremiah.

"And none of the farm went to you in the divorce?" Willow asked.

Marisol took a step forward. "I wouldn't dare, and whoever told you I tried to take that farm from him is lying," she snapped.

Sydney held out a hand, placing it gently on Marisol's arm to calm her.

Willow cringed and said, "Sorry, that's none of my business. I just narrowly avoided marrying a man who definitely would've become an ex-husband, and I don't like to see women taken advantage of in situations like that."

"It's okay," Sydney said softly. "It's a touchy subject for her."

Marisol held up a hand to show that she really was okay. "Jeremiah's family owns the farm, actually. It was there and running long before he and I got together. Plus, things with our divorce were already combative enough. I didn't want to add trying to take a piece of the Pine family land to the list of offenses people were building against me."

Even though Marisol used the plural, Lou got the distinct feeling she was mostly worried about the opinion of one person. But who was it? Surely not Jeremiah, if they were divorced. Right?

Lou stepped forward, checking over one shoulder before saying, "Marisol, we're not trying to besmirch your ex-husband's name, but we heard he fought with the state auditor that we found dead in the middle of Willow's nursery. You wouldn't know anything about that, would you?"

Marisol eyed her warily.

"If we can solve this, and my nursery can open, I have a whole selection of locally grown, healthy plants that I would be happy to sell in your store," Willow added.

That seemed to sweeten the deal, because Marisol eyed Sydney and said, "I can't help you much with the details. We've been divorced for six months now, and I don't know his day-to-day schedule or hear about the people he interacts with anymore." Just when Lou was giving up hope, Marisol added, "But I can tell you that the man had a terrible temper. It was part of the reason I left him. He never took me seriously, but I warned him that if he kept giving in to his anger, someday he was going to hurt someone."

Lou digested that information silently. "Do you know of anyone else who might know more about Jeremiah's conversation or schedule?" Lou asked.

Marisol turned to Sydney, who said, "Lowell, he's my ex-husband. And he works with Jeremiah."

Willow snorted. "You're not serious."

The women nodded in tandem. "They got the farm, and we got the garden center."

"And do you think Lowell will talk to us if he's so loyal to Jeremiah?" Lou voiced the concern itching at the back of her mind.

Marisol burst into laughter. Sydney's cheeks turned red.

"Oh, no. I mean, Lowell is loyal to Jeremiah to a fault. He would never tell you anything that could hurt him." Sydney cut the air with her flat palm. "But he's also incredibly terrified of getting in trouble with the law. If you tell him Jeremiah might have gotten himself into trouble, he'll spill everything."

"Same with Jeremiah," Marisol added. "He usually won't talk, but if you threaten him with lawyers, it'll either make him spill everything or he'll get mad as a hornet."

Willow rubbed her hands together, as if she were equally looking forward to either option. "Perfect. Thank you."

"We'll be in touch," Lou said with a wave as Willow paid and they headed out for Jeremiah Pine's farm on Dill Drive.

Just as Marisol had described, the Pine family farm was not only beautiful, but sprawling. Peggy Lee's farm, where Willow's stock was being grown and harvested, was tucked in the crook of a rolling hill, getting just the perfect amounts of sunshine and shade. Jeremiah Pine's operation made Milner Farms seem like a suburban backyard.

Willow let out a low whistle as they pulled up to a farmhouse with a circular driveway. A few trucks sporting the decals for Pine Landscaping sat along the side of the house —a fleet ready to make any customer's landscaping dreams a reality.

A man peered out of a small barn next to the main house. From what Lou could see inside, it was where they stored their tractors and different heavy equipment. And given his big uncertain posture and swiveling gaze, he didn't appear to be the owner. He must be Lowell.

Willow strode forward and said, "Excuse me, sir. We're here investigating the death of the state agriculture auditor, Harley Bramble. We've heard that your employer Jeremiah Pine got in a heated argument with the man mere days before his death. What can you tell us about that?"

She impressed Lou. Willow not only managed to talk fast and confuse Lowell, but she seemed to channel Easton and his cop energy. She'd never actually said they were law enforcement but from the way she held herself, Lou was pretty sure Lowell thought they were, from the sweat forming on his brow.

"I ... this ... I can't." Lowell took a rag covered in dark, oily stains and ran it along his brow. "I know that the auditor was here last week. He left Jeremiah a citation, but I'm not sure what it was for. Jeremiah doesn't always tell me th—"

"Lowell." The name was barked out like a warning from a police K-9.

Jumping, the women turned around to find a tall man striding toward them from the other side of the driveway. He wore a tacky, tropical button-up T-shirt, shorts, and sandals that seemed wholly unfit for landscaping work. Even though he wasn't dressed for farmwork, the way he held himself told Lou it had to be Jeremiah, just as she'd been so sure of Lowell's identity.

It was interesting to Lou how much these men looked like their ex-wives. She could immediately tell that Lowell had lived with Sydney and Jeremiah with Marisol.

"Who are you?" Jeremiah asked, appraising Lou and Willow as he came to a stop in front of them.

Lou thought about Marisol's pointers. Lowell had started to spill information when he'd thought they were cops, so it was worth a try to make Jeremiah think they were lawyers. "We're from the offices of Henry, Grey, and Sapphire." She straightened her posture, hoping that would make her sound more lawyerly. Again, she didn't say *law* offices, so she wasn't exactly lying.

The briefest of smiles flitted across Willow's face as she caught onto Lou's plan. She cleared her throat. "We've got questions about the argument you had with State Auditor Harley Bramble last week at the work site of one of your clients' homes."

Lowell, who had been sure the women were detectives, frowned as he changed that guess to lawyers. His confused gaze ping-ponged between his boss and the women.

"What do your offices care what my argument with him was about?" Jeremiah set his jaw.

The determination in his stance manifested as frustration in Lou as she realized he would not budge. Willow, apparently, had a different reaction to his attitude.

"Sounds like something a guilty person might say," Willow snapped, setting her own jaw to match his.

His face turned the approximate color of a freshly cooked beet. "You have no right to call me that. Mr. Bramble and I were having a professional disagreement."

"Dad?" The name was barked out in the same warning tone Jeremiah had used with Lowell. This time, however, a young woman was the one addressing Jeremiah.

She looked to be in her twenties, wore rubber boots, and a bandanna covered most of her brown hair that wasn't pulled up into a bun. She came striding out of the house. Lou didn't miss the large shotgun propped up on the covered porch, but the woman walked past it.

"Stop talking, Dad. These women are just about to leave." She held the self-assured stance of George. Lou had thought that level of self-assuredness at such a young age was something unique to George, but this young woman obviously exuded a similar amount of gravitas.

Willow seemed to agree with Lou's assessment of the young woman because she held up her hands and backed away. They left, but once Lou had turned out of the farm driveway, she pulled off to the side of the road.

"Well, Marisol was right about the hornet part." Willow puffed out her cheeks. "She just didn't mention that it was her daughter that would do the stinging."

And I think I solved the mystery of whom Marisol was so worried that she'd let down, Lou mused to herself. If Jeremiah's daughter was also Marisol's daughter, and she worked for the farm, maybe it was Marisol who was on the outs in the family.

"Did you see his shirt?" Willow asked.

Lou squinted. "Yeah, a Margaritaville shirt?"

Willow nodded. "Not just any Margaritaville shirt. One specifically from Key West."

Lou tried to remember why that was significant. "Where the toxic tree that killed Harley grows," she said as it hit her.

Willow swallowed. "We may not have gotten much information out of him, but we know he's got a temper bad enough that he might hurt someone, and he's visited the area where the murder weapon was grown."

"What are the odds of that?" Lou asked rhetorically.

"Pretty darn slim," Willow answered anyway.

CHAPTER 10

Willow and Lou spent the ride back to Button in silence. Lou's mind was working out what everything they'd just encountered meant, and from the way Willow was chewing at her lip, it was safe to say she was doing the same.

"You want me to come over? We could do lunch," Lou said as she dropped Willow off at her place.

Easton must've seen Lou's car pull up, because he came out of his house to greet them.

Willow reached out and squeezed Lou's hand. "I'm okay. Easton's here, and I was thinking I might drive out to Milton farm and hang out with Peggy Lee and Beau. Thank you for spending the morning with me. I'm going to fill him in on the Jeremiah situation and see if we can't get Roy looking in that direction."

Lou smiled. "Anytime."

Willow opened the door, but before she could get out, Easton placed his forearm on the doorframe and leaned in to greet them. "Good news," he said in lieu of a standard hello. "They're done searching the nursery, and they didn't find so much as a seed of those prohibited plants."

"That's great." Lou beamed at Willow.

Willow blinked, as if in disbelief. "Virginia said that would be the only way they could make any charges stick against me." The sentence was like one long exhale. Lou could see some of the worst of Willow's fears leave her in that moment.

On the heels of that good news, Lou waved goodbye and headed home. She made a detour, stopping at the clinic to check on the cat from earlier. The waiting room was empty, and there was a note on the desk that said Kathleen was at lunch and to ring the bell she'd left behind if anyone needed help.

Lou didn't want to bug anyone. She checked her phone to make sure Noah hadn't texted while she and Willow were off on their Brine adventure. About to leave, Lou hesitated as a door opened behind her.

"Hey," Noah's warm voice filled the room, and she turned to greet him.

"I was just on my way by, and I was going to check on the new guy, or girl, but I saw Kathleen's note and I didn't want to bother you." She rambled a little, noticing that she was nervous.

"Nonsense. You're never bothering anyone. Come back and see him." Noah waved her through to the exam room he'd just exited. "We're in between patients right now, so you're not interfering at all," he assured her, seeing the hesitation in her stance.

"Him?" Lou asked as she finally followed Noah.

There was a gleam in Noah's eye as he confirmed the cat was, in fact, a boy. "Got any suitable names picked out?"

Lou pursed her lips. "I have been rereading *The Count of Monte Cristo*. Maybe we should use up Alexander Duclaw." It wasn't as if she could come up with names on the fly like her father, but she kept a list behind the bookshop counter she added to as she thought them up, crossing them out each time she used one for a bookshop cat.

Noah laughed. "Dumas. Duclaw. I like it." He gestured to a small kennel area where she found a gray cat peering out from a crate stacked on top of others, sitting about chest high. "He certainly is worthy of the Alexander name."

"He's great?" Lou guessed, squinting one eye.

Noah snapped his fingers. "I can't ever get anything past you."

She beamed, first at Noah's compliment and then at the cat inside the crate as Noah extracted his large body.

"I'm guessing great mostly describes his size." Lou marveled at how big the feline was. Compared to the small cats she had in her bookshop right now, Alexander was practically a giant. He would make even Charles Lickens seem tiny.

"He's a big boy. Fifteen pounds." Noah lowered and raised the cat as if he were on a set of scales. "But he's healthy and not microchipped."

"That surprises you," Lou guessed, based on Noah's reaction.

Noah nodded carefully. "He's flea free, which tells me he might be on an oral flea medication."

"Which would be a sign that he has an owner," Lou added as she realized what he meant by that.

"Or *had* one." Noah shifted his weight. "We've seen an uptick of people deciding they don't want a pet and just letting it go in a town or two over from where they live. He also doesn't seem to be starving." The cat rubbed up against Noah's hand as he set it down. "Well, for anything but attention. But sometimes strays are really proficient hunters, and they can keep themselves happily fed."

"So?" Lou hesitated, not sure what all of that meant. "Should I take him with me or not?"

Noah ran a hand over the back of his neck. "I would say you're good to take him. I'll have Kathleen keep her ear to the ground about anyone who might be missing a cat, but if he traveled all the way to Willow's, I'd say you're okay."

Together, they packed Alexander into a crate and got him ready to travel back to the bookstore.

Lou spent the first few minutes settling the new cat in the back room, making sure there was nothing blocking the door so the other cats could get used to his smell in the space underneath the door. She opened for the afternoon, given that today wasn't technically supposed to be a day off and she'd only taken it to make sure Willow was okay.

With the intense amount of foot traffic going past her window, she would be wise to capitalize on some of the tulip festival shoppers. They were easy to spot because of the tote bags they carried, citing that they'd visited the Northwest Plants farm. As much as Lou appreciated being able to identify the tourists so easily, she hoped the smaller family-run tulip farms were also getting as much traffic as the large conglomerate.

The moment she flipped the sign to Open, she had a rush of people flooding inside.

"Oh, I'm so glad you're open. I've heard such great things about your shop. I was sad I might miss it."

"Look at all these cats! This is so much fun."

"I'm looking for a good fantasy series. What can you recommend?"

Lou was hopping for the next few hours while she catered to her patrons. A wave of gratitude washed over her as she rang up a long line of customers while another group crowded around the cats, giving them love and attention. She had the best job.

She was tired and ragged in the very best way that evening when she closed the shop. Despite her fatigue, she couldn't seem to get the itch out of the back of her mind. Unsure what it was about, she had a conversation with herself as she cleaned up and did her evening chores in the shop.

"What are you anxious about, Lou?" she asked herself.

"Nothing, other than worrying that Willow's dream of opening her own nursery won't ever come true and that she's going to be heartbroken."

"That's a lot." She pursed her lips. "But it's not what's bugging you. What's really got you scratching your head?"

"It's just it's the third time we've heard them mentioned today."

"Who?" But Lou knew even before she could answer herself.

Northwest Plants. Seeing the tote bags and hearing customers gabbing about the company in relation to the tulip festival *had* been the third iteration of a conversation about the company that day. The first being the flyer she'd seen in the Briney Bean and the second when Marisol had mentioned getting her stock from the company.

Lou wasn't sure what root rot looked like, exactly, but she knew enough to know that the way those plants had been wilting in the front of Marisol's Garden Center, they weren't healthy.

Once she'd moved the other cats upstairs, she gave Alexander some time exploring the shop. She was pleased to see that he knew how to use the cat box when she went to grab him from the office. He was so friendly. But she immediately noticed a few odd quirks about the cat, the first being that he hadn't touched the wet food she'd set out for him. There was a dent in the dry food, but she knew her cats usually preferred the wet stuff if they could get it.

Unsure if he drank any water while she was working, Lou tried putting some of the wet food on top of the dry stuff to see if that would entice him and hydrate him a bit. Meowing, he ran right over and devoured it. Lou narrowed her eyes. Going to the cupboard in her office, she pulled out a third bowl and used it to switch the dry food to the white bowl and the wet food to the clear one.

Feeling like a scientist, she set the clear bowl in front of Alexander. He dove right in.

"Okay, so you prefer clear bowls," Lou said aloud. She'd never had a cat who cared what kind of dish they ate from before, but there was a first time for everything. That settled, she opened the door and let him roam around the shop.

While Alexander Duclaw explored the space, Lou did some research. She looked up verticillium wilt, focusing her energy on the images available as examples. The pictures online looked almost exactly like the ones Marisol had sneered at in her entryway. And while she hadn't named the "big corporation" she was using as a supplier ever since she'd gotten divorced from Jeremiah, Lou had a gut feeling it might be the same Northwest Plants.

Lou came out from behind the computer desk to pace around the bookshop while she thought. If Willow and presumably Jeremiah had both been threatened with citations, fines, and the threat of being shut down, a big corporation would have to suffer the same consequences. Right? It seemed almost more important since they probably did a lot more selling and distributing than small-timers like Willow and Jeremiah.

Alexander came out from between the bookshelves as he noticed Lou pacing. He meowed and walked with her. She was about to tell him how cute he was, when the cat flopped his body onto the floor right in front of Lou. Crying out in surprise, Lou narrowly avoided stepping on Alexander.

"Whoa, little buddy. What did you do that for?" Lou leaned down to make sure he was okay. After confirming that she hadn't stepped on the cat, she added, "That's a dangerous habit you've got there, Mr. Duclaw."

He purred and blinked his golden eyes up at her, none the wiser that if the whole interaction had gone differently, either Lou would've fallen and possibly broken a bone, or he would've gotten the shock of his life when her foot had landed on him.

She scooped him up, ready to give him a talking to about why that was so dangerous. But before she could say anything more, the cat placed both of his paws on either side of her face. Lou was frozen in place, and not just because his claws were extending into the skin on her cheeks ever so slightly. She also wanted to see where this was going. Alexander pulled himself forward until he licked the tip of her nose and moved back, letting his paws drop.

"That was weird." Lou let out an uncomfortable chuckle.

There was a knock at the bookshop door, startling Lou out of her conversation with the cat. Spinning around, she found Willow waiting outside. She placed the cat back onto the floor and ran over to open the door.

"I thought you were going to the farm to be with Peggy Lee and Beau." Lou stepped back as she let her friend inside.

As Lou closed the door and turned toward her friend, she found Willow pacing through the shop, much like Lou had been doing moments before. Lou's eyes shot to the gray cat as he rolled onto his feet and darted over to walk with Willow.

"Watch out!" Lou called, pointing to the cat just as he flopped his body directly in front of Willow's pathway.

Willow, stunned by Lou's outburst, screeched to a halt, curling her body back as far as she could to stop her forward movement. She just missed stepping on the happy gray cat, who exposed his belly and rolled on the floor as if he hadn't a care in the world and hadn't almost just been stomped on by a human.

"Yikes!" Willow called out, taking a couple of stumbling steps back. "That's a dangerous stunt, little sir." She wagged her finger in front of the cat, who followed the movement with his eyes like she might be playing with him.

Lou walked over, scooping him up off the floor. "Alexander Duclaw is quite the quirky guy, I'm realizing. He almost made me fall doing the same thing moments before you arrived."

Willow blew a stray hair out of her face. "That's probably not going to go over too hot with the customers, especially not the older ones."

"Yeah." Lou cringed. "I thought about that as my life flashed before my eyes."

Falling now that she was close to forty was a lot scarier than it used to be when she was in her twenties and could bounce back. A fall now might mean weeks of soreness or even an injury. And from what she knew from her parents and her older customers, it only got worse as one aged.

"But I'd feel awful having to lock him away. Trapped in that back room most of the day is no way to live." As Lou spoke, the cat wriggled around in her arms, moving so he was facing her. With his two paws, he placed them on her cheeks and licked the tip of her nose again, just as he had before Willow had shown up.

"Well, that's sure cute." Willow tilted her head as she watched the display.

"It would be cuter if he weren't using his claws to hold his paws steady on my cheeks." Lou flinched in pain. "Okay, if we stand still, I'm going to let him down again." She let the large gray cat slide out of her arms and onto the floor, where he continued his tour of the bookshop. "Sorry about that tangent. You came over here in a hurry. What's up?"

Willow blinked as if remembering what had brought her there. "Oh, right. Easton and I were doing a little weeding, and it hit me: Northwest Plants has the disease Harley Bramble was worried about. The one he told me would prevent me from opening. I didn't recognize it right away when we were in Marisol's store, because I was pouting and then overwhelmed by how much good stuff she had, but those sad plants at the front of her store, the ones that must've been from the big distributor, were dying of verticillium wilt."

Smiling, Lou said, "Great minds think alike." When Willow frowned in confusion, Lou motioned for her to come see what she'd been searching for on the bookshop computer. After making sure there were no gray cats underfoot, Willow moved to check and smiled as well.

"And if Harley was trying to give them a citation, I'm guessing the fine attached to it was a lot larger than the one he was about to give me."

Lou tapped her nails on the counter. "Which would definitely be motive for murder."

CHAPTER 11

"State audit records have to be public, right?" Willow twiddled her fingers in the air above the keyboard. "We just have to know where to look." She lowered her fingers, but no sounds of clicking followed.

"And you don't know where that would be," Lou guessed.

Willow shook her head, frowning.

"Neither do I." Lou chewed on her lip for a moment before snapping her fingers and saying, "What about George?"

"Yes, George will know." As if the techie young woman was already there, Willow stepped out from behind the register.

"I'll see what she's up to," Lou said as she pulled out her phone.

Internet search question/help needed. You free?

Lou knew not every citizen of Button could get such a quick response from George, but Lou was special. George hung out at the bookshop almost every day it was open. She'd become a very good friend to Lou over the past year. So it did not surprise her at all when George texted back almost immediately.

> Just finishing a level. Be over soon.

"She's coming," Lou informed Willow. She gestured for them to sit at the round table so they could talk.

"So how's Alexander Duclaw, besides trying to break your neck?" Willow glanced around the shop for the cat, but he wasn't anywhere they could see at the moment.

"He's good." Lou smiled. "Weird, but good."

"How so?"

"He only eats out of clear bowls, does that nose-lick thing, and flings himself in front of walking people. I'd say those are pretty weird habits," Lou scoffed.

"True. Maybe they're things you'll get used to." She didn't seem hopeful as she grinned at Lou.

"What about you? How are you feeling?" Lou asked. "Honest three?" It finally seemed like an okay time to ask, since Willow'd had time to think about the situation and had gotten the boost of the good news from Easton about the prohibited plants.

Willow inhaled, holding on to the breath for a beat before releasing it. "Worried. Hopeful. Scared." She let out a wry laugh. "I'm not sure exactly how I'm staying hopeful and worried, since those two things seem mutually exclusive, but I am. I'm worried it's going to affect my business, but I'm hopeful it won't." She shrugged.

"I think that's a great attitude to have about it all." Lou definitely felt encouraged by her friend's response. The fact that there was even one positive adjective on that list after the past twenty-four hours was a miracle in and of itself, in Lou's opinion.

The door opened, surprising the two even though they'd been expecting the young woman who walked inside a moment later.

"Hey," George said. Her brown hair, which was usually in a messy bun on the top of her head, was currently gathered into two space buns, making her look like she was from one of the manga books she liked to read. "So you've got an internet search quandary for me." George glanced toward the computer and wiggled her fingers, much like Willow had minutes before, but this time the action wouldn't end there. George would know just where to look.

Lou and Willow filled her in on the situation. They told her that their top suspects were Jeremiah Pine and Northwest Plants, or someone who represented the company and had recently been to town.

George walked over to the computer. But on her way, Alexander Duclaw skirted out from underneath the table, unbeknownst to either Lou or Willow. He'd found a new person to meet, and he raced over, flopping down right in front of her, just as one of her boots headed for his body.

"Nooo," Lou called out, feeling like it was all happening in slow motion. She even had time to scold herself for not putting Alexander away before George arrived.

But just before George stepped on the cat, she jumped with her other foot, sending her body up in the air while she pulled her arms in and twirled like an ice skater, doing a 180-degree turn before landing a few feet away from Alexander.

Lou dropped the hand she'd been reaching toward them onto her pounding chest. Willow collapsed forward onto the table as if the stress had sapped her of all her strength.

"That was close," Willow said from where her face was buried on the table.

George knelt to pet the new cat. "That was *fun*."

Willow and Lou shared a dubious look and then turned back to watch George scratching the cat's belly.

"Who's this?" George asked, having not been privy to the story about how they'd found him or that he was a stray who needed a home, but at that point, it was implied.

"Alexander Duclaw," Lou explained. "He's new and a little quirky."

George's eyes lit up as she turned to Lou. "How so?"

Lou laughed. "I mean, you saw one of the things he does right there. He loves to walk next to you and then randomly throw his body in front of your feet. I can't figure out how he's stayed alive this long with a favorite pastime like that."

George scratched under the cat's chin. "That's just him trying to keep people on their toes. I like it."

Lou remembered George saying something about starting up parkour, a sport that was about randomly jumping and rolling. Maybe there was climbing involved too? Regardless, it had sounded like just a little too much for Lou and her almost forty-year-old bones. She would stick to long runs, thank you.

"He only eats out of clear bowls," Lou added, flicking a second finger up to show George there was a list.

George nodded as if that was a normal cat behavior that made sense to her.

"And if you pick him up and let him face you—" Lou started, but George didn't wait until Lou finished, to try it.

She scooped up the massive cat, pressing him to her chest and holding her arm under him for support until they were face-to-face. Alexander put his paws on George's cheeks and then licked her nose.

"Omigosh, that's the cutest thing I've ever seen." George swooned as she held him closer to her.

Lou's eyes went wide. Not only did this seem to be George's dream cat, but he also couldn't be trusted in the bookshop, and Lou wasn't sure what she was going to do with him tomorrow when she had to be open for a full day.

"Do you want to try him out?" Lou asked. "No commitment is necessary. Just see if he works out at your place."

Hugging Alexander closer to her chest, George squealed happily. To cement the fact that he was the perfect cat for her, Alexander only purred louder as she jumped around in excitement. It was good that he was okay with loud noises. George often played video games during the day and was known for shouting at the screen when something surprised her or one of her virtual teammates wasn't doing what they were supposed to.

"They're perfect for each other," Willow said in awe as she observed them.

"I didn't hear exactly what you said, but if it wasn't that we're perfect for each other, I don't want to know," George called from the other side of the room. Kissing the cat on the head a few times, she put him down and focused on the computer.

Lou couldn't help but adopt the same wide smile George was sporting as she browsed. It seemed finding Alexander Duclaw had put her in a great mood. Lou hoped that meant she would be even more focused during the internet search they needed her to do.

George made a clicking noise with her tongue as her fingers flew across the keyboard and expertly guided the mouse across the desktop.

"Do you know what Harley's auditor number was?" George asked, glancing up quickly. Seeing blank stares answer her back, she said, "No problem, I just have to go to one more place and … yep. Got it. The security on some government websites is a joke."

Lou stood. Willow threw an arm out to stop her.

"You're not doing anything illegal on Lou's computer, are you?" Willow asked tentatively. "I don't want her to get in trouble because she's trying to help me."

George shot Willow a sympathetic look. "Aww, that's sweet. No, don't worry about it. I'm using a VPN to block your IP address at the same time that I'm bouncing it around to confuse anyone who might be watching. For all they know, I'm getting into their system from the middle of Montana. Oh, now somewhere in Iowa. And now it's in Florida." Her cheeks flushed with color, showing she was entirely too happy with herself and the power she held over computers.

The clicking halted, and George leaned close to the screen, reading quickly as her right fingers used the mouse to scroll down the page.

"Bad news. Northwest Plants does not have root rot or that wilt thing you talked about in their stock." Her eyes flicked right and left across the screen. "Harley visited their local warehouses three times over the past month and cited concerns about verticillium wilt. But he wrote a note on … the day he died." George's gaze cut suspiciously over to Lou and Willow.

"That might've just been a coincidence," Lou said slowly.

George's fingers flew across the keys again, and she wielded the mouse as if it were an ancient weapon she'd spent years training how to use. Her eyes widened.

"I think Lou's optimism might be right this time," she reported, pointing to the screen. "Your boy, Jeremiah, has been cited"—George's lips moved as she counted—"thirteen times." But that wasn't even the worst part. George continued her narration as she clicked on the most recent citation. "The most recent one was last week, and Harley wrote a note here that Jeremiah told him to 'get stuffed.'" George used finger quotes around the phrase.

Lou gulped, wondering if the toxic apple stuffed in Harley's mouth counted.

"What was the citation for?" Willow asked, curiosity leaking from her tone.

George scrolled back up and peered at the screen again. "Not the presence of a disease, like you might think. Jeremiah had planted a super toxic and not at all legal tree on a client's property. Something about machines and eels?" George shook her head as she tried to read the auditor's notes.

"Manchineel tree," Willow whispered. If Lou hadn't remembered which tree that was, Willow's next sentence cleared it up. "See? I told you he'd been to Key West, and that was trouble."

George clapped her hands together. "So, what do we do now?" She grinned. "Are we going to Brine to find this dude and bring him to justice?"

Lou and Willow shared a worried glance, but Willow said, "Actually, I don't think we need to do anything. I already told Easton about Jeremiah and how guilty he seemed. He texted Roy, and the guy was receptive to looking into him tomorrow, said he already had him on his radar, so you know, it was already his idea." Willow rolled her eyes. But all three of the women knew better than to take Roy Anderson's approval for granted. It wasn't ever going to be perfect, so they took what they could get.

"Seriously?" George's shoulders sank forward. "After all that intrigue? Nothing? I'm just going to take this adorable cat home with me, and we're going to let the professionals handle the rest?"

Lou nodded. Willow did too.

George blew a raspberry and gave them a thumbs-down. She strode around the computer desk and register counter, toward the office. "I'm borrowing a crate, Lou," she called as she rummaged around in the office.

A few minutes later, George left with Alexander Duclaw in tow. Lou sighed, both the weight of the case and the dangerous cat off her shoulders.

"What do we do now?" Willow asked.

"Want to get some ice cream?" Lou's eyes sparkled. If it was wrong to have a s'mores sundae two days in a row, she didn't want to be right.

CHAPTER 12

The scents of cream and sugar greeted them along with Ribs.

"Ladies. Evening." He inclined his head as if they might be royalty. "What brings you here tonight?"

Honestly, Lou felt like a queen as she ordered a s'mores sundae and Ribs told her to have a seat. Choosing the table closest to the ice cream counter, Lou waited until Ribs was scooping the ice cream into the sundae dish before saying, "That friend of yours in Brine, the one who overheard Jeremiah and the dead auditor arguing last week..."

Ribs stopped what he was doing to show he was listening.

"He wouldn't be the kind of client who's very hands-on and knows every plant on his property, would he?" Lou waited for the answer.

As if he'd expected her question to be much harder than that, Ribs nodded and continued to scoop ice cream. "Oh, for sure. Francis knows everything that goes into the soil on that property. He's really into plants, just doesn't like to—you know—plant them." He wheezed out a laugh.

"So if there were a very dangerous tree that wasn't native to the area, he would've … asked for it specifically?" Lou chanced the guess.

Ribs considered her question. "Something dangerous sounds a lot like Francis. He loves things that can almost kill him." Ribs looked right and left, even though they were the only people in the shop at the moment. "I love the guy, but he's so rich that he's at that point where he's just buying stuff no one else can afford because he can. He's definitely the kind who might hunt people, just once, just because he could."

As inflammatory of a sentence as it was, Lou recognized the allusion to the old short story about rich men hunting people. "So maybe he asked Jeremiah to buy one and plant it on his property." Lou glanced over at Willow.

But Willow was busy staring at her phone. "Sorry, I'm just checking the prohibited species list here on the Department of Agriculture's website." After a few seconds of reading, Willow shook her head. "It's not on the list. It's not prohibited to buy or sell in the state of Washington. They probably figured they didn't need to put it on there because only a fool would want to plant one of those on purpose."

Ribs brought the sundae over with a flourish of his hands. The sugar on top of the marshmallows was still bubbling from being hit with the torch. He handed over two spoons and told them to enjoy.

They did, especially since everything was clicking into place. Jeremiah had a conflicted relationship with the victim. He also had access to the murder weapon.

"And he probably has bolt cutters somewhere in that big barn of his," Willow said, making sense of how he'd gotten inside Valley Nursery's gate to kill Harley.

It all made sense. So why did Lou still have a terrible feeling in her gut when she thought about the case?

THE NEXT MORNING, Lou opened the bookshop at her regular time. As much as she was glad to have been there for her friend during a tough time, Lou loved her routine.

She loved getting ready, then having the small parade of cats follow her down the staircase into the bookshop. After giving them food and making sure their downstairs litter boxes were clean, she would get started on some coffee for herself.

Once the clock struck eight, there was usually at least one cat fast asleep in a morning ray of sunshine as it filtered in through the large front windows of the bookshop. That morning was no exception. Sapphire and Anne Mice were curled up together on one of the fleece beds that Noah and his daughter, Marigold, always sewed for the new foster felines. Lou made a note to text Noah when she got a chance to tell him to take the one he or Marigold made for Alexander to George's house, but she also didn't want to jinx the match, so she held off until she figured out how their first day together had gone.

Two of Lou's regulars waited out front when she came over to flip the sign in the window and unlock the door.

Silas, a man who lived in the assisted-living complex down the street, came daily to get his cat fix since he wasn't allowed pets in his apartment. Catnip Everdeen couldn't wait to jump up in his lap the first chance she got once he tottered in, placed his bowler hat on the arm of the love seat, and settled in.

Forrest was also waiting that morning, meaning he probably had an early client and had a little time to kill before his next one. The local psychologist was a lovely mixture of calm and rational that Lou appreciated. His wife, while not deathly allergic, couldn't handle a cat living in their home, so she made do with the few random hairs he brought home after spending time at Whiskers and Words.

"Willow staying out of jail?" Silas asked, never one to mince words.

"I had Gianna scratch her from the list for this evening." Forrest grimaced. "I hope that was okay. We just figured she would have enough on her mind." He eyed Lou. "We weren't sure about you, however."

Lou blinked. The list? That evening?

"For Pete's sake, the duckling fundraiser," Silas barked out at her, making her jump. "It's tonight."

That evening's fundraiser was a play on the classic children's story, *Make Way for Duckling* by Robert McCloskey. It was called Bake a Tray for Ducklings and required all participants to bring a unique traybake to the high school gym that evening for a modified cake walk. Lou was pretty sure one of the local kindergarten classes had come up with it since the new teacher was British and traybake was more of a UK phrase. But she didn't mind. She had her trusty lemon-bar recipe on hand and knew it would be a winner.

She had completely forgotten about it with everything else going on. But even though she had a lot on her plate, she wanted to help. Ever since moving from the Big Apple to a town as small as a Button, she'd really surprised herself with how much she enjoyed the small-town events and fundraisers. Lou was sure her donation to the fundraiser wouldn't be needed, knowing the town's fondness for the baby ducks, but she wanted to be involved.

"Keep me on the list. I've got just the recipe. Any word about how the little babies are doing?" Lou asked Forrest, remembering now that Gianna was on the planning committee.

His brown eyes brightened. "They're thriving. Gianna and the others were extremely concerned at first. A water-fowl expert told them ducklings that age usually have much more time with their mother, and when they're separated it usually means certain death. I think the fact that we found them so soon after their mother disappeared helped."

Lou swallowed. "So there's still been no sign of the mother?"

Forrest shook his head.

"That darn coyote that's been terrorizing everyone's chickens probably got it. That and Willow's little goat, I'm sad to say," Silas said, actually sounding a little sad for once.

"No. Steve is too big and grumpy for a coyote." Lou

refused to believe that. But she hated that there was a hint of doubt behind her definitive statement.

Before Forrest could chime in about his thoughts on the coyote, the bookshop door opened, and the last of Lou's regulars entered. She honestly hadn't been expecting to see George that day now that she had a feline friend at home and all. And while she wasn't upset to see her friend, she was … confused.

"What in blue blazes is that?" Silas just about spit in his haste to comment.

Normally, Lou didn't find a lot to side with Silas about, but she had to admit, this was kind of exclamation worthy. Even the unflappable Forrest gaped as if he wasn't sure what he was seeing.

Fabric was wrapped around George's body, zigzagging in front and behind her, crossing over her shoulders and knotted in the front. It was like one of those newborn baby wraps that Emily had used with Lou's nieces when they were young. Actually, it wasn't *like* one of those. It *was* one of those wraps.

Where Emily used to place Maddy and Mia, George had tucked Alexander Duclaw. The wrap supported his bottom and his back legs. His front paws hung out the top as if he were lying in a little cat bed, and his head rested on her collarbone. He was fast asleep.

"This one's gone from zero to one hundred on the cat-lady scale in a matter of hours." Silas pinched the bridge of his nose.

Having been someone who'd always embraced the cat-lady term, Lou shot him a look of disapproval. She didn't want Silas shaming George. There was already enough stigma going around about women who liked cats, as it was.

There had to be a good explanation for what they were seeing.

"Is everything okay with him?" Lou asked, worry engulfing her as she realized maybe George had him like that because he was injured and couldn't walk.

George beamed. "Oh, Geralt? He's great."

Lou recognized the name of the main character from *The Witcher* books and the video game by the same name that she knew George played.

"I just got tired of holding him all the time," George explained. "My neighbor gave me this when she noticed me struggling. Her youngest is in school now, and she said she doesn't need it anymore." The young woman shrugged and scratched at Alexander's head.

He barely blinked before drifting back off to sleep.

Lou checked with Forrest and Silas tentatively before saying, "You know you don't have to hold him *all* the time, right?"

It wasn't as if George was new to cats. She spent time at the bookshop most days. Lou didn't go around carrying Sapphire everywhere with her while she worked. He would usually curl up with her in the evenings or come rub against her shins, meowing to be picked up every once in a while throughout the day, but he was pretty independent for the most part.

George snorted. "Oh, *I* know that. Try telling it to him. To be fair, he wanted to sit with me while I played video games, and I guess I move a lot more than I realized. Between aggressive controller movements, jumping up when things get intense, and crossing or recrossing my legs, I'm not a very good lap. This way, my hands are free and he's just with me for the ride." George gestured to the cat in the baby wrap.

A grin peeled across Lou's face. It was an explanation, and it really wasn't up to Lou to decide whether it was a good one. George seemed ecstatic and Alexander Duclaw—now Geralt—seemed more content than any cat Lou had ever seen.

"Plus, with this I get to take him with me as I walk around town." George moved farther into the bookshop, plopping down on the couch across from Forrest.

And even though Silas was still scowling—in fact, his glare might've gotten even more pronounced as she explained everything—Forrest was grinning just like Lou. That made her feel better. If the psychologist wasn't worried about George's mental health or emotional well-being, then Lou wouldn't waste any energy fretting about it either.

"Are you coming to the fundraiser tonight?" Lou asked, picking up the conversation where they'd left off before George had arrived.

George nodded. "I'm making salted caramel brownies." Turning to address Forrest specifically, she added, "Let Gianna know that I'm free after three if she needs help with setup."

"I will do that. Thank you." Forrest dipped his head, still smiling at the purring, sleeping cat in the wrap.

George sighed and looked around. "Well, I guess we're going to continue our morning walk." She stood and waved. "I'll see you all tonight."

With that, George and Geralt left, walking out into the sunshiny spring morning. Lou, Silas, and Forrest gaped after the pair, wondering what it was they'd just witnessed.

CHAPTER 13

Later that afternoon, during a lull in the shop, Lou texted Willow.

> How are you doing today? Also, are you going to the duckling fundraiser tonight? I'm baking lemon bars if you want to come help or take half credit. Forrest said Gianna took you off so you wouldn't feel obligated.

She waited, loving the sound of the birds singing outside. Spring was one of Lou's favorite seasons. She didn't care if it was cliché, but she loved the promise it brought after months of cold and drab winter. The green shoots breaking through the soft earth meant so much more after seeing so much brown for months. The warmth of the sun felt even more delectable after being cold for so long. And the birds' happy chirps and elaborate songs sounded even sweeter after the quiet slumber of winter.

The flowers on the forsythia shrubs outside her shop showed off a brilliant yellow, looking like pieces of sunshine that had dropped from the sky.

A gray minivan pulled up outside the bookshop. A gaggle of tulip festivalgoers bundled out of the vehicle, waving and saying thank you to Martie. It seemed like the Ryde gig was going well for the woman. Lou was happy for her, knowing she'd had a hard time keeping a job because she was also her elderly father's caretaker and couldn't work steady hours in case he needed her. Lou waved to Martie through the window as the woman pulled away in her van, probably on her way to pick up more tourists.

The group she'd dropped off filed into the bookshop holding the telltale totes from none other than Northwest Plants. Lou had still been so new last spring, she'd almost been too overwhelmed with everything else to pay much attention to the amount of tourism they got from the large farms to the north. This year, she and Willow had gone driving around to see the fields of colorful flowers during the first week in April, before the crowds got too bad. And Lou could see the draw. Somehow, even after seeing rows after rows and fields after fields of tulips of every color, she still wanted to see more. With the small roadside farm stands, she could see why it was an annual favorite for Pacific Northwest families and visitors alike.

Lou loved every customer who stepped foot inside her bookstore, but the tulip tourists were a special breed of shoppers. They weren't just there to spend money, which was always a plus in Lou's mind, as well as any other business owner, but they were ... how could Lou describe it?

Whimsical. Seeing the tulips and sipping on farm fresh juice, eating a salad made with local greens and fresh fruits, and knowing they had jars of homemade jam in their tote bags, wrapped up next to handmade wood-fired pottery adorned with tulips, to commemorate their experience, made them whimsical in a way that Lou hadn't seen before. They were the spring equivalent of the fall-leaf peepers, fully immersed in the "vibe."

And if that meant going to a town as cute as a button after their tulip trip and splurging on books they'd "wanted to read for so long," then Lou was happy to be a part of the event.

"Excuse me," one of the women in the large group said as she approached Lou. "I heard there was a nursery in town, but the only one we saw on our way in was closed."

Lou's heart sank, knowing Willow had wanted to capitalize on some of the tulip tourism, which had been yet another reason behind her opening this week. Pushing through her momentary sadness, Lou reminded herself that it was only mid-April. Willow still had plenty of time to open before the tulip crowds would be gone. But it reminded her that the case of the murder of Harley Bramble needed to be wrapped up in order for that to happen.

"I'm so sorry. That is the only one in the area. It's my best friend's place, actually. She just hit a little snag and won't be able to open for a few more days," Lou explained.

The woman's face brightened. "Your best friend?" She placed a hand on her chest. "Aww, that just warms my heart. Well, if you talk to her today, tell her we just love that troll of hers. Such a fun addition. We may have stopped and gotten a picture with him." She giggled and glanced over at her group of friends, who followed suit.

Lou suppressed a chuckle of her own. Peggy Lee might've been right after all. She would have to let her know, even if it meant hearing "I told you so" from the ornery older woman.

Once the women purchased their books and left, Lou checked her phone again. Willow had responded.

> Oh good. I'll have to thank Gianna for that. Yeah, making something might've been one too many things for me today. I'm definitely coming, but I might just meet you there. I've got a lot to do today. Lots of movement on the case. I can't wait to fill you in.

Excitement surged through Lou at the text. Movement in the case was good. And Willow sounded positive for the first time since Friday. It sounded like they'd been right about Jeremiah after all. With one less thing to worry about, Lou finished out her last few hours of the day in the shop and then wandered upstairs with the cats to work on her traybake.

Starting with the shortbread base, Lou got that baking in the oven while she worked on the lemon curd. Her favorite part was pouring the bright yellow curd over the lightly toasted cookie bottom before popping the whole thing back in the oven. Lou returned to the book she'd been reading while she waited, reveling in the sweet, tangy, springy scent that filled her apartment as the bars baked and cooled.

She showed up at the high school gym just a couple of

hours later, looking like everyone else arriving with a long tray of baked goods held in front of them, like an offering. She joined the line for check-in, surveying the space as she waited with the others. Those who'd wrapped theirs in clear cling film were subject to having to answer questions about the different flavors and toppings inside. The ducklings, stars of the event, were in a pen with a kiddie pool and some hay in the center of the space. Lou had to admit Forrest was right. They *were* thriving. She was glad to see it.

Stepping forward every few minutes, Lou finally made it to the front. A woman with long dark hair pulled back into a ponytail sat behind the check-in table. "Welcome! Sign in with me, and then you can see Betty to my right if you'd like to buy tickets."

Lou filled out her name, the type of baked good she'd brought, and wrote in any allergens in the last column. The woman turned the clipboard around, checking that all the information was correct as she placed the corresponding number on top of Lou's traybake.

"Oh, you're Louisa Henry," the woman said with a smile, placing a hand on her chest. "I'm Carly Zimmerman. I took over the horticulture position here after your friend Willow left."

"Right." Lou *had* heard that name before. "It's great to finally meet you. How are you liking the job?"

She chuckled. "I'll admit. It's a little tough being in Willow's shadow, but it's good. We're figuring things out."

The woman behind Lou cleared her throat in a thinly veiled reminder that there were other people in line. With a wave, Lou stepped to the right to pay for a round of tickets, as well as an added donation to the ducklings.

Once that was done, Lou went to read the sign hand-written by one of the high schoolers. It explained how the ducklings were found and that the money raised today would create an enclosure and a small pond for them in Button Memorial Park so everyone could enjoy the ducks, and they would be safe from the local wildlife.

Lou knew through Forrest that there was a small contingent of locals who'd wanted to set them free in Button Lake or even Master's Pond up by Willow's nursery, but Gianna and her fellow volunteers convinced them they'd already handled them too much, and while their interference had likely saved their lives, it had also domesticated them. It would just be cruel to put them out into the world.

Greeting people as she walked through, Lou perused the different traybakes that had been donated. Hers was actually one of three lemon bar bakes. She marveled at some of the more adventurous flavor combinations. Some were less complex in flavor but held more intricate designs on the top.

Lou's feet came to a stop as she spotted something a few traybakes down. Was that traybake decorated with a gray goat? Someone had piped the word "Missing" above the gray animal. Lou's heart pounded loudly in her chest. Confusion whirled around inside her as she tried to make sense of what she was seeing.

She knew Willow wasn't submitting a bake, so either someone had taken it upon themselves to decorate their traybake that way for her sake, or they were possibly making fun of Willow. While one option was sweet and thoughtful, the other was so much the opposite.

Stepping nearer, Lou's confusion only grew. On closer examination, she realized it wasn't a goat at all, but a cat. A gray cat. The red letters of the word "Missing" seemed like a warning now that Lou was up close. Her heart sank. The white tail, two white socks, and small white eye patch were somewhat crudely created out of frosting. Now that she was up close, Lou recognized the gray cat. Alexander Duclaw was, in fact, someone's cat, Buttons.

As a person who came up with clever cat names all the time, Lou experienced a small amount of judgment pass through her at the idea of naming a cat Buttons in a town called Button—not very creative, if you asked her. She peeked at the name on the card in front of the bake to see who'd done it. The sick feeling in her stomach only grew more terrible as she read the name Bella Greene. Bella, as in Roy's new girlfriend, whom they'd had that disastrous dinner date with the other night.

A groan built in Lou's throat.

"Well, this isn't good." The deep voice surprised Lou as a man sidled up next to her. She immediately relaxed upon seeing that it was Noah.

"I jumped in too quickly, letting George take him." Lou grimaced. "We talked about the possibility that he had an owner, and I was blinded by how well George got along with him."

"Especially after how many cats she's tried," Noah said, seeming to understand Lou's eagerness.

Somehow, knowing that Noah understood still didn't

make the reality any easier. "It's going to break her heart to give him back."

"I'll talk to George when she gets here. Don't worry." He placed a hand on her shoulder, but it did nothing to ease the knot of tension between her shoulder blades.

Neither did seeing her best friend enter the gym a moment later. Excusing herself from Noah, Lou trotted over to meet Willow so she might keep her away from the decoration that looked a little too much like a goat—Bella really didn't have the best frosting skills. She didn't want Willow to see it and get her hopes up without reason.

"Hey, how's it going?" Lou stopped in front of her friend.

Willow eyed her warily. "Why'd you rush over here like that? What's wrong?" She peered around Lou, searching for whatever it was her friend was trying to keep her from. The woman knew Lou too well.

"You said there had been a lot of movement on the case," Lou said, improvising. "I'm just eager to hear what that is."

Willow's eyes lit up as if she'd forgotten until that moment. She grabbed on to Lou's arm and pulled her over toward the far wall where they wouldn't be overheard. "Roy actually listened," she said, jumping up and down a few times. "He went to question Jeremiah today."

Lou couldn't believe the words she was hearing. "He did?"

"He did." Willow nodded, seeing Lou needed more reassurance. She wrinkled her nose. "I mean, he went into his office and did some digging of his own after Easton talked to him, but *then* he decided it was worth checking into, so I call that a win."

"I do too."

Any happiness Lou felt at the news disappeared as a gasp cut through the gym. In the time Lou and Willow had spent chatting about the case, George had arrived.

She stood stock-still in front of the missing-cat traybake, a hand over her mouth. When she turned to face Lou, there were tears in her eyes.

CHAPTER 14

The only saving grace in the whole mess was that George hadn't worn Geralt there in the baby wrap. That would've made an already awkward encounter even worse.

It was terrible enough.

Lou raced forward, reaching George at the same time Bella Greene did.

"What's going on? Have you seen my cat?" Bella's gaze flicked from George's face to Lou's. Recognition flashed behind her eyes and they narrowed, proving that she definitely remembered Lou from dinner the other night.

George, normally stalwart, sniffed as a tear fell down her cheek. Lou wrapped an arm around her shoulders.

"I'm so sorry," Lou said. "We found him loose in a field, and he seemed like he needed a home. We checked, and he wasn't microchipped."

Bella placed a hand on her hip. "Are you blaming *me*

here? You're the one who took someone else's cat and *gave* it away."

Lou *had* been trying to make Bella feel bad for not having her cat microchipped. But the anger cleared from her mind, and she shook her head. Bella was right. "I was. I'm so sorry. I should've waited longer and asked around first before assuming."

Lou hadn't come across this before, mostly because her fosters were usually there for a lot longer before they were adopted. George and Geralt hitting it off so quickly had been a surprise and one that had caused Lou to make a spur-of-the-moment decision that was now causing someone she cared for pain.

"I'll expect him back by tonight." Bella lifted her chin until her nose was up in the air and turned on her heel.

Lou turned to George, moving her side hug into a full embrace as the younger woman cried into her shoulder.

"Oh, George. It's all my fault. I'm so sorry." Lou patted the woman's back, sending a few waves toward people passing by who hesitated like they wanted to help. "Do you want me to walk home with you so I can come get him?"

George sniffed. "Sure. I think it'll be better if you take him. I don't think I'd be able to go."

Lou agreed. It was the least she could do after she'd created the terrible situation.

"But can you wait a few hours to show up?" George asked, a small flicker of hope in her eyes. "She said tonight, and it's only four. Do you think I could spend a last couple of hours with him first?"

"I think that will be fine," Lou said, squeezing George's arm. "I'll text when I'm on my way to your place later."

George ambled through the gym doors toward her house. Lou felt like crumpling. Willow was by her side in a moment.

"That was awful," Lou complained through a groan.

"It was hard to watch for sure." Willow cringed.

As if that had reminded her that there were other people around, Lou noted that almost all the eyes in the place were focused on her and Willow at that moment. They'd all seen and heard.

"Why don't we head out?" Willow steered Lou toward the door.

Lou hesitated, worried about missing the activities. But they'd already paid for their tickets, so they'd taken part monetarily. That would have to be enough. Lou didn't want to be the object of everyone's pitying or judging looks anymore.

She and Willow walked back to the bookshop toward where Lou's car was parked. They were just rounding the corner of the bookshop building when they noticed a truck parked in front. The decal on the side identified the vehicle's owner as Pine Landscaping.

"Omigosh." Willow yanked Lou back around the corner and then flattened herself up against the building. "Did Jeremiah come to get revenge on us for telling Roy about him?"

To Lou's panicked mind, that sounded like just what was going on. She scooted to the edge of the window on that side of the building, peering through it until she could get a better but still hidden view of the truck. The problem was, windows worked both ways, and Lou wasn't as hidden as she thought she was, especially not since the person was already peering through the front windows and immediately caught sight of her.

"It's not Jeremiah," Lou said, jerking back toward Willow. "It's his daughter, and she's coming our way." Pushing Willow away, Lou moved toward the back of the building.

"Hey, stop!" Brynn yelled as she rounded the front, shoulders tensed and fingers curled into fists.

Lou checked over her shoulder and was about to run when someone else shouted, "Hey, yourself!" George strode across the street, Geralt in a cat carrier at her side.

Brynn whirled around, glancing at George, the cat carrier, and then back at Lou and Willow. The confusion on her face made her look marginally less frightening for a moment.

"Why are you shouting at my friends?" George reached the sidewalk and set down the carrier, folding her arms in front of her. The young woman seemed more intimidating in that moment than Lou had ever seen her.

Lou gaped at the two of them, reminded of how similar she'd thought they were upon first meeting Brynn.

A muscle in Brynn's jaw jumped. "They—you." She pointed at Lou and Willow. "The police brought my dad in for questioning today."

George cocked an eyebrow. "So? How's that their fault?"

Brynn's confidence seemed to return as her anger did.

"It's pretty strange, then, that they were there the day before asking the same questions and making similar accusations."

Willow cleared her throat and raised her hand. "I merely told the detective on the case about Jeremiah's fight with Harley," she told George more than anyone else.

But Brynn was the one who responded. "Yeah, and now they're crawling all over the farm."

"If your dad's innocent, then it shouldn't matter, should it?" George said.

Brynn stamped her foot. "It shouldn't, but it still does. We live in a small town. People talk. Even the police coming to our house was enough to lose Dad a client this week. They said they don't want to be caught up in *drama*."

All three of the Button women softened a little in sympathy. They knew that downside of small-town life all too well.

"So you came here to threaten two middle-aged women?" George asked, her nose wrinkling in disgust. "What was your plan?"

Brynn's fingers relaxed from the fists they'd been clenched into. "I don't know. I was just mad, and I drove here. I went to her nursery first, but it's not open, so I came here." She jabbed a finger toward Willow.

"Well, make a better plan next time, one that doesn't include us." George took a step toward Brynn.

The two young women sized each other up for a moment. Brynn shoved her hands in the pockets of her zip-up sweatshirt, digging around until she pulled out a set of keys. Something fell out of her pocket as she pulled out the keys, but it appeared to be trash, so Lou stayed quiet as she stormed off toward the truck. Lou was glad to see her leaving, and she didn't want to do anything that might stop that from happening.

The truck kicked up a plume of exhaust as Brynn stepped on the accelerator and zoomed out of town, much faster than the twenty-five-mile-per-hour speed limit.

The moment the rumble of the truck's engine faded into the sounds of birds chirping in the spring evening, Lou, Willow, and George all sighed in relief.

"Thanks for coming to our rescue," Lou said, giving George a salute.

George let out a wry laugh. "No problem. It gave me a momentary outlet for my frustration and anger."

Willow mumbled, "We could've taken her without the kid."

But Lou walked over to inspect whatever fell out of Brynn's pocket. And even though it turned out to be trash, it was very specific garbage that Lou had seen before in the last few days.

"Is that another gum wrapper chain?" Willow's voice, all bravado just moments ago, trembled with fear.

"Why do you sound so scared about that?" George asked warily.

Lou swallowed. "There was one of these on the ground just near the body they found in Willow's nursery. We think it might've fallen out of the killer's pocket."

"Oh," George said. "Yeah, that is scary, then, because that means ..."

"That means Brynn might actually be the murderer in

the Pine family, not Jeremiah." Despite the warm sun beaming down on them, a chill wound around Lou. She motioned to the bookstore, pulling out her keys. "Let's head inside so we can talk."

Once inside Whiskers and Words, George set the cat crate on the table. "Should I keep him inside?" she asked Lou.

"Yeah, let's keep him in there." Lou scratched at her cheek as her mind worked on recalculating her understanding of the case with this additional evidence. "I think I'm going to need to pace in order to dispel some of this adrenaline from that encounter, and I don't want to worry about stepping on the little guy."

Willow stood behind the register, and she leaned her forearms on the check-out counter. Her gaze drifted off into nothingness.

"Brynn's protective of her father and the family business," Lou reasoned aloud. "She would have access to the same plants as her dad, so even if they only had one of the manchineel trees, she would know which property it was on if she wanted to take a branch with a piece of fruit."

"She obviously makes chains of discarded gum wrappers, just like we found on the body," Willow added. "And did you hear her say she stopped by my nursery? I don't think this is the first time she's been there. She knew about me before we showed up at her family farm yesterday."

George snapped her fingers. "Which means she might've also stolen Steve."

Lou and Willow froze as they realized the same thing at that moment.

Grabbing her keys from her purse, Willow said, "That's it, we have to go back. We have to see if she's keeping Steve on that farm."

"Hold on." Lou held up a hand to stop Willow. "We can't just follow her back and go barging through their land. We could be arrested, or worse." Lou shivered, thinking about the large shotgun she'd seen propped up on the covered porch. She wasn't sure if it was for critters or trespassers, but she didn't want to find out. "Plus, you keep forgetting that we have an inside man."

"Who?" Willow and George asked at the same time.

"Marisol," Lou said, disappointed that her cool statement needed so much explanation.

"Oh, right." Willow bobbed her head as she thought about it. "Right." She smiled as she saw Lou's plan. "Marisol is Jeremiah's ex-wife and Brynn's mom, we think," Willow said, explaining to George. "She owns the garden and hardware shop in Brine, and we hit it off right away."

Lou pressed her lips together, not sure if that's exactly how she'd describe their first meeting with Marisol, but she felt like the woman would help them. "Listen, I've got to take Buttons here to Bella's place," Lou said the statement carefully, watching George take in every word. "But then Willow and I should make our way to Brine so we can make it before Marisol's store closes."

George nodded, only tearing up a little as she peered over at the gray cat in the carrier, showing that she was coming to terms with the difficult situation.

"I'll wait here with George," Willow said, shooting Lou a look that told her she would make sure George was okay.

Lou grabbed the cat carrier and went out the back door into the alley between her shop and the clothing boutique. Once she got the carrier and Buttons in the back seat, Lou pulled out her phone and texted Noah.

> Is Bella still at the fundraiser?

If the sour woman was still there, Lou was going to drop off the cat with her there, in front of half the town. If she'd already gone home, that was fine too.

> She left a few minutes ago. She's probably home now. You taking the cat?

> Yeah. George just dropped him off. I want to do it quickly, so she doesn't have to say goodbye more than once.

> Thank you for doing that. Sorry I didn't catch her before she saw the cake.

> No worries.

She put away her phone and drove toward the Greene residence that her map app pulled up, just past Willow's farm a few streets. Even though it was in the same general area of town, that cat would've still had to travel a long way to get to Willow's house.

Lou parked in front of a small farmhouse and a barnful of chickens. She pulled in a deep breath and readied herself for the encounter.

CHAPTER 15

Lou didn't even make it to the porch before Bella opened the door and strode out, a big grin on her face and arms outstretched. The problem, from Lou's point of view, was that she wasn't sure if the smile Bella wore was the joyful expression of a person being reunited with a family pet. To Lou, it seemed a lot more like the smirk of someone who just won a sneaky hand at poker.

"Buttons, I'm so glad you're back, baby." Bella knelt next to the crate first, jabbing her fingers through the holes in the metal door. She pried the handle out of Lou's hands with a glare, pulling the cat toward her.

"I know it's none of my business, but microchipping is a great way to ensure your pet doesn't get lost again." Lou cleared her throat.

Bella stood, letting the carrier drop with a thud to the earth. It was only a few inches, but the clamor scared the cat, who braced himself in the center of the crate.

"Oh, don't worry. Noah already did without my permission when he did the exam." Bella narrowed her eyes. "And he already gave me a lecture at the fundraiser tonight about how Buttons needed vaccines since he's under a year old. I've been taking care of animals my whole life. I know what to do if they get sick."

Lou had powerful feelings opposing most of what Bella was saying, but she knew fighting with her about it wouldn't change her mind. Plus, she needed to get back to the bookshop so she and Willow could head to Brine to find some answers about Steve.

Just as she was about to leave, a cottage on the edge of the property caught her attention. It was gorgeous, a lime green that Lou normally wouldn't have gone for, but surrounded by plants as it was, it looked like a secret cabin in a storybook garden.

The switch in her focus hadn't gone unnoticed by Bella. "That's Carly's place. Zimmerman?" The way Bella said the last name made Lou feel stupid that she hadn't known it right away.

"Oh, the woman who took over Willow's horticulture classes at the high school." Lou snapped her fingers. "Right. I met her tonight at the fundraiser. She seems nice."

"We're actually best friends." Bella's voice held a lot more tension than Lou thought the situation warranted, as if Lou merely commenting on Carly's house meant she wanted to steal her away as a friend. "She just moved in a year ago, kind of like you."

The words, "Only better" weren't voiced, but Lou could feel Bella thinking them.

"Good for you," was all Lou could think of to say. She

hitched a thumb toward the cat carrier. "You can bring that back to me at the bookshop anytime you have a chance. I have a few more just in case I need to transport anyone else in the meantime."

Bella knelt down, opening the door right there in the front yard. "You should just take it now. I won't remember to bring it to you otherwise." Sticking her hand into the crate, she pulled out the cat, giving him a weird pat on the head before shooing him off toward the barn. "There. Don't run away this time."

Lou gritted her teeth. She needed to leave now, or she was going to steal that woman's cat again. She couldn't imagine just tossing him outside again after she'd already lost him once. And for a woman who'd decorated an entire traybake with the cat's likeness as an edible missing poster, she didn't seem to care that he was back. Lou grabbed the carrier, turned on her heel, and headed for her car.

She couldn't make eye contact with either Bella or the cat as she backed out of the long driveway. Shedding a few tears on the drive back, Lou made sure she composed herself before stepping foot back in Whiskers and Words, knowing George wouldn't make it if she were crying too.

Luckily, George didn't ask about the cat handoff or about what kind of welcome home Buttons received. She simply said, "Ready for Brine?"

Lou glanced at Willow in question. "Oh yeah. We're bringing George with us."

"I'm too sad to stay home tonight. I need something exciting to do." George's shoulders moved up, close to her ears in excitement.

"Trespassing on someone's land, searching for a stolen goat is definitely exciting," Lou muttered to herself, feeling a little more trepidation about the plan than the other two seemed to.

"Plus, Brynn seemed mildly scared of George, so I figured she'd be an excellent addition to our team in case we run into her again." Willow grabbed her purse.

Lou followed her out the back door. "If we run into Brynn again, I'd say we'll have bigger problems, namely jail time."

George nodded. "Then let's try not to get caught."

Lou sighed. If only it would be that easy.

During the drive to Brine, the women planned out their strategy. They would approach Marisol first, seeing if she had any insider way onto the property without breaking the law or where they might keep an animal in one of the many barns. If Marisol knew nothing or wouldn't help, they'd be on their own.

"There were like six barns on the property, though. That's the tricky part." Willow stared out the window at the passing scenery.

"And Steve could be in any of them." Lou squeezed her eyes shut for a moment, letting herself experience the overwhelmingness of the situation.

"Maybe this Marisol character will know if we can deduct any from our searching radius." George held up a finger. "Deduction is the way to solve all mysteries."

"You reading Sherlock Holmes or something?" Willow checked over her shoulder at George sitting in the back seat.

In the rearview mirror, George grimaced. "Not reading. I'm watching this old series on the BBC with that guy who plays Dr. Strange."

Now it was Lou and Willow's turn to wince. Old? Lou didn't think of the Benedict Cumberbatch version of *Sherlock* as old at all.

Lou didn't push the issue about George calling the show old or preferring to watch instead of read. George had always been open with Lou that reading wasn't her favorite thing. She preferred comic books to chapter books and was surrounded by stories with her weekly Dungeons and Dragons group, as well as the elaborate story lines from her video games. Lou had learned over the years that everyone digests stories differently, and that was okay. She never wanted to shame anyone for their choice in how to experience stories.

George hung back as they entered the garden center a short while later. Willow and Lou walked straight to the check-out counter where Marisol stood instead of Sydney.

"Back to make that deal?" Marisol cocked an eyebrow at Willow.

Holding up a hand, Willow said, "Not yet. We need your help."

Marisol put a hand on her hip. "You do? I thought you got what you wanted. I heard a Button detective came to question Jeremiah today."

Willow nodded. "This is personal. I think my goat is on that farm."

"Your goat?" Marisol coughed out the question.

Willow glanced at Lou. In the car, when they'd made the plan of what they would, and wouldn't, say, they'd agreed that bringing up Brynn or their suspicion that she could be the actual killer was a bad idea. They'd all felt strongly that she wouldn't help them if she knew they suspected her daughter.

"It's a long story," Lou said, jumping in. "We just need to know where your ex-husband might keep an animal like a goat on the farm, and if you know of an easy way for us to sneak onto the property."

At that moment, George wandered over to them. Marisol's eyes latched on to the young woman. Her expression, which had been wrinkled in confusion, softened at the sight of George.

"Can I help you find something?" Marisol asked in the most maternal way. Lou practically expected Marisol to follow that up with an offer to make George a snack and ask her how her day at school was.

George pointed to the women. "Oh, I'm with them."

Marisol blinked at Lou and then Willow. "Is she your daughter?" The word daughter sounded strangled as it came out.

Lou frowned. Willow sucked in a breath.

"Omigosh, you *could* be my moms." George tapped her fingers as she did the math in her head.

"But we aren't." Lou stepped forward. "She's our friend."

Willow glared at George as if that might not be the case any longer if she continued to call them old.

"Oh, you wanted to know about which barn to look in." Marisol shook her head, as if clearing her thoughts. "The only one fit to keep any livestock in would be the big white one on the southern edge of the property."

Lou cringed. That had been the one closest to the house.

Marisol waved. "Don't worry about Jeremiah. He sleeps like a log. Never woke up once during all the years our daughter cried in the middle of the night." The admission was bitten out in a tense sentence.

Lou kept it to herself that they weren't actually worried about Jeremiah hearing them.

None the wiser, Marisol kept going. "There's a house on the other side of the barn. It's blue, and you have to go past the farm and take a left to get to the driveway. Park there and you can sneak into the barn from there."

Willow opened her mouth as if to protest.

"No one's there right now." Marisol held up a hand. "It's Sydney and Lowell's old place. After the divorce, Sydney moved in with me, and Lowell moved into the apartment above the machinery barn. They're selling the place, so if anyone asks why you're parked there, just pretend that you're waiting for the Realtor to show you around. Her name is Polly."

That would've worked a lot better if Jeremiah, Brynn, and Lowell hadn't all seen them before. But Lou thanked Marisol all the same and left.

"We have some time to kill until it gets dark," George

said, checking the time on her phone as they piled back into Lou's car. "Want to get dinner?"

Willow huffed. "What kind of dinner could we possibly get around here? Pickles?"

Lou motioned toward the other side of the road. "There's that pizza place we saw last time."

"There's also a diner down the street." George shrugged.

Willow's stomach grumbled in response. "Fine," she said. "Let's get pizza. It'll be less likely that they'll try to put pickles on it."

Lou and George shared a sly smile in the rearview mirror before Lou pulled out onto the road and took the first turn into the next parking complex, stopping in front of the pizza place. They went inside for dinner, which was delicious and completely pickle free.

Once it was fully dark, they drove to Lowell and Sydney's old house, parking in their empty driveway. The house looked sad, all the lights off, no life inside anymore.

"Okay, let's go," George whispered as she climbed out of the car and tiptoed toward the big white barn.

Lou and Willow rushed to follow her, closing their car doors as quietly as possible. They used their phone flashlights to navigate the uneven terrain in between the house and the barn, but Lou felt safe. From that vantage, at least they couldn't see the Pines' farmhouse. The barn created a sort of wall in between the two residences so they had some privacy.

By the time they reached George, she was already inspecting the humongous rolling door that opened the whole side of the building, with her flashlight. It held a padlock and wouldn't budge. Willow checked the smaller door to the right. It opened.

They scurried inside, taking a moment to get their bearings. It seemed like it was used for hay storage at one point or another. Now it just held a few bales in one corner. It was basically empty. There wasn't a goat there at all.

Someone behind them cleared their throat. The three women turned around slowly, pointing their flashlights toward the ground so they wouldn't blind whoever was standing behind them. Well, they had a pretty good idea who it was.

Brynn stood there just inside the barn door, arms crossed, her expression even more furious than from the last time they saw her.

CHAPTER 16

"Please don't call the cops on us," Lou pleaded with Brynn before she could even say a thing. "We're just searching for Willow's goat, and you said that thing about knowing where her nursery was and we got curious. We couldn't help ourselves."

"That seems to be a pretty big theme between the two of you." Brynn glared at George. "Or should I say three?" Then her gaze cut behind her to Sydney's old house where Lou had parked. Brynn's anger melted away into something unreadable for a moment. "Or more than three … who told you that you could park there?"

Willow pressed her lips together, not wanting to implicate her newfound friend and business contact.

"Your mom told us." George stepped forward. "Also, why don't you talk to her? The woman practically looked like she was going to cry when she saw me today because you and I are around the same age."

Brynn ran her tongue over her teeth in discomfort. "It's all a stupid misunderstanding."

"What kind of misunderstanding?" George asked casually, as if they had nothing better to do than listen to her family issues.

Lou couldn't tell if George was trying to buy them time or earn Brynn's trust, but she was going to let George run with her plan, since she couldn't think of anything better.

"I'm sure you heard all about the divorce if you've had a conversation with her." Brynn rolled her eyes, the motion so exaggerated there was no way they were going to miss it even in the dark, with only flashlights to see by.

"She mentioned it," Lou confirmed.

"Well, she's the one who asked for it, and then she was trying all of this shady stuff, asking her lawyer these questions about the property and the land, like she was going to take some of it when it's my dad's family's land." Brynn spoke quickly, everything falling out as if she'd either never been asked or had never answered truthfully until that moment.

"And you don't think she deserves a place to live?" Willow asked, jumping to Marisol's defense.

Brynn's gaze snapped over to Willow. "She got one. The house she's in now is one she and my dad bought together when I was first born, when my grandma and grandpa still lived here and ran the farm. They rented the old house out once we took over the farm about ten years ago." Brynn snorted. "Dad gave her that place free and clear. He just said he didn't want her to come after his family farm. That was the deal."

The Button women listened, sensing that wasn't the end.

"Then her lawyer asks these questions about parceling out the property, and, well, I got angry." Brynn's shoulders tensed. "So I went to her shop and gave her a piece of my mind … or five." She winced. "It was bad. I called her a lot of terrible stuff. Half the town heard. The half that wasn't there knew within the next hour."

"But she wasn't trying to go after the land, was she?" Lou asked, remembering how quickly Marisol had corrected Willow when she'd mentioned the farmland.

Brynn shook her head. "I mean, she was, but it was for me." The last word in the sentence was almost a whisper. "She put it in the divorce terms that Dad had to decide what percentage of the farm I owned, and she wanted him to designate a parcel on the eastern corner where I could eventually build a cabin." Brynn wet her lips.

"Did you apologize?" Willow scoffed.

Brynn's eyes flashed up to meet hers, but unlike the last time, they didn't hold the same fiery energy. "I didn't know how I could take back all the terrible things I'd said, so we just … haven't spoken."

Lou's heart broke for Marisol. It was obvious that she wanted nothing more than to be close with her daughter, but she was trying to give her the space she needed.

Surprising everyone, Willow said, "That sounds like how I might've handled that same situation, honestly."

"Willow knows all about that kind of relationship." Lou stepped forward, then sent an encouraging look back to Willow, waving her forward. "She and her mom butted heads for a lot of her twenties."

Willow nodded. "It was terrible for a while."

"Did you ever go without speaking to her?" Brynn asked, a fat tear dripping down her nose.

"Only a few months, but it seemed like forever," Willow answered. "It turned out she felt exactly the same as I did. We were both too stubborn to see that we both wanted it to end."

"How did you … end it?" Brynn asked.

Willow exhaled a sharp laugh. "My dad made us sit in the living room together one day and said he'd block anyone from leaving until we figured out whatever was going on between us."

"So, you really don't have my goat?" Willow asked. Even though they'd searched the place, it seemed as if there was still the tiniest bit of a doubt in Willow's mind, and she had to put it at ease with the question.

Brynn shook her head. "I don't have your goat. And I didn't kill that auditor either. Neither did my dad."

The three women from Button crossed their arms in front of their chests.

Brynn put up her hands. "The police don't think we did it, either, because we both have alibis. I'm sure they're checking them, since they haven't been back."

"So why did you come to my bookstore to threaten us?" Lou frowned.

"I told you. I was mad, and I wanted to take out my frustration by yelling at someone. The two of you seemed like the best possible candidates at the time." She glanced down at her shoes. "Exactly like I did with Mom. I didn't think about the consequences or whether I'd be able to take back anything I said. I just did it."

"I blew up at people a lot when my mom and I were going through our rough patch," Willow said. "I understand."

"Thanks." Brynn lifted her gaze. "And, for what it's worth, if someone took one of my pets, I think I would break into a thousand barns to find them too." She rocked back on her heels. "Do you three want to come inside for some tea or … I don't know, wine?" She chuckled.

"We would love that," Lou answered for the group.

They didn't have anywhere else to be. George had said herself that she didn't want to be alone that evening. What was better than making a new friend?

"Isn't your dad going to have a problem with that?" Willow asked cautiously as they made their way out of the barn, toward the main house.

Brynn waved a hand toward them. "Dad went to bed an hour ago, and he sleeps like the dead. He won't even know you're here." She led them the rest of the way.

Lou was glad to see the shotgun on the porch had been moved, hopefully locked away for the evening. Any sense of foreboding left her as she stepped into the cozy farmhouse.

Once inside, Brynn heeled off her boots and padded into a large kitchen. Lou and the others followed suit by taking off their shoes while Brynn pulled a bottle of wine from a holder on the countertop and opened it. She poured them each a small glass.

"Have a seat." Brynn gestured to a gray couch in the living room as she sank into an impressive gaming chair that looked a lot like the one George had in her house back in Button.

The chair sat in front of a desk that held a monitor larger than Lou had ever seen, as well as a plethora of technological items that lit up in different colors. The mouse glowed purple, while the keyboard flashed every color of the rainbow, and the monitor was rimmed in a pink light. Her immediate thought was that all those flashing, pulsing lights would give her a headache. George raced forward, checking out the unique items on Brynn's desk.

"Sweet setup." George's reaction was completely opposite from Lou's, as if proving their age difference yet again that day.

"Thanks." Brynn beamed.

The two launched into a few minutes of conversation full of computer terms neither Lou nor Willow understood.

They seemed to get the hint that they were confusing their other companions, because Brynn said, "I can't believe you thought I could've murdered that guy, with a manchineel tree to boot." She scratched at her temple. "Dad told Mr. Knight they were super dangerous, and he was out of his mind if he wanted one on his property, but he wouldn't listen."

"To be fair to you, we had little to go on, so our suspect pool was rather small. We may have been grasping a little." Lou held up her thumb and index finger so there was just a little gap between them.

Brynn pulled her legs up under her in a cross-legged position. "Tell me what you've got. Maybe I can help."

"Well, you already know about Harley Bramble," Willow said.

Brynn chewed on her lip. "Kinda intense about his job, but overall, a nice guy."

"Was a little too liberal with that citation book of his, if you ask me." Willow rolled her eyes.

"Yeah," Brynn said. "Except I think he definitely used it as more of a threat than anything else. There was one time he came and told Dad he was going to get a fine for using pesticides that his client insisted he used, but when I checked, he hadn't actually filed anything."

"Checked?" Lou asked. "Is there a place you can check online?" She instantly felt silly for asking George to hack into their system if there had been an easy and legal way to check on citations.

Brynn's cheeks turned slightly red. "Uh, I mean, there is, if you know how to get past their site security, which is ridiculously easy," she added quickly, as if they might judge her.

Lou, Willow, and George shared amused looks before bursting into laughter.

"What?" Brynn asked, not understanding the joke.

"George did the same thing for us." Willow pointed.

Brynn relaxed. "Omigosh, I feel so much better." But her relief quickly changed to intrigue. "What were you looking up?"

"The stock your mom got from Northwest Plants looked like they had the verticillium wilt that Harley was citing people for lately, and we wanted to make sure he was holding the big companies to the same standard as the rest of us," Willow explained.

Brynn flinched slightly at the mention of her mother. "And was he?"

Lou shrugged. "He had cited them for having evidence of verticillium wilt in their stock, but the citation was later resolved, so it seemed after he tested their plants that they weren't actually carriers of the disease."

But even though Lou and the others had found that to be a fairly settling piece of news, Brynn sat up straight, like she'd just heard bad news.

"Or … and hear me out … is there a different reason the citation went away?" Conspiracy flashed behind Brynn's eyes. She set down her wine, spun around in her chair, and woke her computer, illuminating that expansive screen. After a few moments of typing and clicking, she said, "Ah, here it is. So, one of the first places I got access to was Harley's email account. I glanced around and didn't see anything that pertained to my dad or our farm, so I mostly dismissed it, but now that you mention Northwest Plants, I remember there being something…" She scanned the screen and clicked on a link.

Willow, Lou, and George leaned forward in anticipation, sipping their wine as if they were watching a mystery movie and they'd just gotten to the part where the characters were figuring out how the clues fit together.

Brynn poked a finger at the screen. "His boss, Tessa Delaney, sent him an email about Northwest Plants. She wrote they had gotten a new rig and that Harley should go see a show."

"Um…" Willow squinted one eye. "That still doesn't make sense."

But it did to Lou. "They work for the government, which means their email can be opened to the public if there's enough cause behind releasing it. She's writing in code. I think that's her telling him they're too big, and he should let it go."

"Like Cockney?" George asked. When everyone turned in her direction, she added, "You know how they rhyme things instead of saying what they really mean."

Brynn nodded. "That makes sense. But here's the part that is most interesting. Tessa signs off the email by saying he should try for someone else's job."

"He wanted her job?" Willow asked.

"And she sounds threatened enough to take action against him," Brynn said.

"But why would she kill him at my nursery?" Willow asked, distraught.

Brynn clicked around. "Let's see." She worked for a moment before raising an eyebrow and saying, "It could be this email Harley sent her last week complaining that you were belligerent and churlish. He describes the fight he got in with you about the verticillium wilt and how you swore your plants were fine."

"So I was just a scapegoat for her." Willow tapped her fingers on the arm of the couch. "Did he also let her know he would be at my nursery that evening?"

"Emailed his entire team," Brynn said.

Lou inhaled sharply. "So not only does Tessa have a motive to kill Harley, but she had the opportunity because she knew where he was going to be and knew by leaving him in Willow's nursery, she would become the prime suspect." Lou frowned. "Does she have access to a manchineel tree?"

Brynn scoffed. "She sure does. Harley emailed her about the tree Dad planted at Francis Knight's property. She would've just had to swing by and grab what she needed to poison Harley and then meet up with him at Valley Nursery that evening."

"Is Francis rich enough that he has a security system?" George asked, sitting up straight.

"I think he has three." Brynn's eyes sparkled.

CHAPTER 17

Ribs hadn't been joking when he called Francis Knight eccentric. The man lived in a palace … in a town named after pickle juice.

Huge metal gates enclosed the driveway, so cars couldn't get in, but a fence did not accompany them, so someone could just walk around the outside and gain access to his grounds.

"Seems futile." Willow shook her head as they stopped in front of the gate, and Brynn punched the button on the intercom.

"Yes?" The voice on the other end sounded like a stereotypical movie butler. "Ms. Pine, we have not requested landscaping services tonight, have we?" he asked genuinely, as if night gardening was something his eccentric owner might realistically request.

"No night gardening," Brynn said, barely containing a giggle. "We've got a bit of a mystery we were hoping we could get Mr. Knight's help with, and—"

The enormous gates swung inward before Brynn had even finished her sentence.

"He's very excited. He'll see you in the parlor." The butler sounded even less emotional than before.

They drove forward, toward the expansive and hulking building. The place looked like it could've been transported from India, especially with all the exotic plants crowding the space.

"Your dad maintains all of this?" Willow asked, her question engulfed in a gasp.

Brynn nodded proudly.

"He must really know what he's doing to keep these alive in the Pacific Northwest." Willow gaped at the tropical assortment of plants.

Brynn turned off the engine and said, "The trick is that Mr. Knight is richer than a king, and he buys special heaters to keep the plants happy during the colder months and a watering system more expensive than my entire farm to keep them properly humidified." She rolled her eyes as if it were the silliest thing she'd ever heard. "But he's also one of my dad's biggest clients, so I don't care how crazy he is."

Now that Lou was there, she kind of got Ribs's hunting-people reference. What was that short story back when she'd been in school? *The Most Dangerous Game* by Richard Connell? The rich men hunting people had seemed so out of this world, but now Lou could place the story here and could see it all in her mind. A shiver raced down her spine.

They walked up to the front entrance, flanked by gorgeous burbling fountains. Lou could've sworn a tropical bird squawked somewhere in the bushes. The entryway was arched, made from two doors like a castle. They were both pulled open at once, and a butler in standard livery stood in the entrance. He bowed forward and motioned for them to come inside with the wave of a white glove-clad hand.

The floors were a gorgeous hardwood that was polished to an immaculate shine. They held the most intricate grain, a mixture of dark and light woods like a loaf of marbled rye. Another, larger fountain took up the space within, and the place was decorated with dark woods and stone. A staircase wound up to the second story to their left.

But the butler signaled for them to walk to the right. They followed him into a room that looked like they had fashioned it after one of those fancy secret men's clubs back in the day.

A man wearing a merlot-colored, velvet smoking jacket with a white ascot sticking out of the collar sat perched on a barstool along what had to be the most expansive home bar setup Lou had ever encountered.

"Ladies," the man crooned. "To what do I owe this pleasure? I heard something about a mystery."

Brynn, the only one who'd actually met this Francis Knight before, stepped forward. "Good evening, Mr. Knight. Yes, we—"

Knight held up a finger, stopping Brynn. "I don't mean to be rude, but I think it would be even more so if I didn't offer you and your friends a drink first."

Glancing over her shoulder, Brynn checked with the women from Button. Lou wasn't sure she trusted this man yet, and they'd just had a little wine at Brynn's house. They didn't need anything. She shook her head, hoping it was okay that she was answering for both Willow and George too.

"No, thank you," Brynn answered.

He let the hand he'd held up to stop her float back down to the counter. "Very well, then. You may continue."

"We need your help with a mystery," Brynn explained. "It's about a man who died on my friend Willow's property, and she and my dad are now the primary suspects."

The man lifted an eyebrow over his bored eyes. "Ah, yes. The state agriculture auditor. I know all about it."

"From whom?" Lou asked before she could stop herself.

He gave her a wink. "I pay people to keep me informed of the goings-on in Lakeside County."

"Do your people know who killed Harley Bramble?" George asked.

Francis Knight chuckled, but he didn't answer her.

George widened her eyes at Lou and Willow in a look that asked, *Should we be here?*

Brynn seemed unfazed and not intimidated by the man, because she walked forward. "As you probably know, they killed the auditor using repeated exposure to the parts of the manchineel tree."

Francis cocked an eyebrow. "He had one of the small apples in his mouth. His hands were covered with boils as if he'd touched either the toxic branches or gotten some of the sticky white sap on his fingers. And his autopsy showed that he had recently inhaled the toxic smoke that comes from burning the manchineel tree bark."

Lou and Willow shared an impressed but still scared look. How did he know all of that?

As if he could read their minds, he said, "Again, I have people I pay to keep me in the know."

An icy fear settled over Lou as she realized that the reason this man might know so much about the way the auditor died was because he was the one to kill him. Lou had to remind herself that this was just Ribs's army buddy Frank, who'd come into a lot of money and was all about living it up, not about hurting people.

"We think the person who killed him used your new manchineel tree as the murder weapon." Brynn crossed her arms, getting down to business.

Francis's eyes lit up. "And you want to see my security footage? Good idea." He stood. "Follow me." He waved lazily as he moved from the bar toward the front foyer once more.

He walked across the foyer to the room on the opposite side of the bar, then took a right. Turning on the light, he illuminated a home theater room. It had a tiered floor, so the back seats were a few feet higher than the front ones, and each of the large leather recliners were staggered in the space so each person would have a direct view of the huge projection screen at the front of the room.

"We're watching a movie?" George asked, stopping at the top of the tiered platform.

Francis *tsked* and waggled a finger at her. "Stewart can send the security feed to this projector. This way, we can watch in comfort."

Lou supposed it was better than trying to peer at a tiny

security screen, which was definitely what she'd imagined when Brynn had brought up checking the feed.

They each chose a seat, all up close to the screen, when the lights dimmed and the projector hummed on, displaying the logo of its manufacturer for a moment before showing them an entire bank of security recordings.

"Okay, what day are we looking for?" Francis asked. Somewhere in the background, Stewart clicked on the date entries and waited for further instructions.

"Well," Lou said tentatively. "He died in the evening last Friday. So the person would've had to come collect the parts of the tree before that. But it could've been anytime before that, really."

"After Dad planted it on the property the Friday before," Brynn reminded them.

And even though it effectively narrowed their time down to a week range, which was much better than months or years, it still felt like a daunting task to search all hours of the day and night for that length of time.

Francis sighed as if he shared Lou's concerns, but said, "I suppose all we can do is start the night he died and work our way backward."

Stewart followed the suggestion as if it were an order. The date and time displayed in the corner, the red numbers were such a stark contrast to the black-and-white night-vision display. Stewart pressed a button, and the time slowly ticked backward. Other than the time moving, they could see the feed was moving because the plants swayed in the wind. Every once in a while, a small animal scurried by or a bat flapped by the screen. Then the sky lightened and darkened again, proving a whole day had gone by.

But just as the sky was lightening a second time, there was a movement on the screen that wasn't an animal. A person appeared next to the manchineel tree.

"Stop there," Francis ordered. The feed froze. "Now, toggle around a few seconds to see if we can get a good look at her."

Lou's heartbeat quickened. He was right. It was most definitely a woman. Her long hair was pulled back into a low ponytail, and she wore a dark zip-up sweatshirt over jeans. Lou didn't know what Tessa Delaney, the director of agriculture in Washington State, looked like, but she was a government employee; it would be easy enough to find her picture online. George's face was illuminated as she pulled out her phone and opened a search window, probably doing that very thing.

But as Stewart clicked forward in ten-second increments, and they finally got a good look at the woman, Lou realized George didn't need to find Tessa's picture. The woman in the feed, cutting off a branch of the tree, was someone Lou recognized.

"Carly Zimmerman?" Willow squinted at the screen as if she couldn't believe what she was seeing.

"Who?" Brynn asked.

"She's the high school horticulture teacher who took over for me when I quit to start the nursery," Willow explained.

George swallowed. "Willow, I think this proves Harley

Bramble's death wasn't about him or the policies he was pushing in his department."

Lou agreed. "This and the disappearance of Steve point to a personal vendetta against Willow."

She placed a hand over her chest. "Why would Carly hate me?"

Brynn sighed. "It sounds like that's what we have to figure out."

CHAPTER 18

As much as it seemed Francis would've preferred they stay there and figure out the rest of the mystery with him—the man really seemed to be lonely in that big house—Stewart reminded him he had an early flight to Japan in the morning and needed to get to sleep. So the women made their way back to Brynn's place.

They talked through the options as they drove.

"She mentioned that it's been rough being in your shadow," Lou said, thinking aloud about why Carly might've wanted to hurt Willow. "Do you think that would be enough to want to get revenge on you?" Lou asked, feeling considerably like it wasn't a good enough motive for goat kidnapping and murder.

Willow raised her hands, palms up. "I mean, it doesn't seem like it to me. I've had students tell me they wish I was still there, but I haven't heard anything bad about Carly specifically."

"Who would have a better idea about what's been going on with her?" George asked.

Lou sucked in a quick breath. "Earlier, when I was dropping off Buttons the cat"—Lou paused, glancing in apology at George—"Bella Greene said that she and Carly were best friends, and they live next to each other."

"Yeah, but Bella's as likely to talk to us as Carly would," Willow said.

"True." Lou's hopeful posture deflated. "What about Principal Henning?" Lou asked.

Willow had adored her principal, saying multiple times how lucky she'd been to work with such a supportive and creative boss. In fact, Flora had been very supportive of Willow following her dream, even though it meant losing an excellent teacher.

"She might know." Willow nodded. "But she's pretty by-the-book, and I doubt she'd say anything that could be misconstrued as gossip. You know who would actually tell us if something was truly wrong? Mrs. Kyle."

The friendly registrar in the high school office would be much more likely to spill the truth than the principal. In her limited interactions with Flora Henning, Lou got the impression that she was a very by-the-rulebook leader and wouldn't share confidential information about one of her employees. It would be easier to get the truth out of someone else.

"Do you know where Mrs. Kyle lives?" Lou asked.

"She's on Pin Street," George and Willow said in unison.

It wasn't a surprise. Willow had worked at the high

school for over a decade, but George had gone there as a student.

Brynn yawned as she pulled into Lowell and Sydney's former driveway, where Lou's car was waiting for them. "As much as I'd love to join you all, I've got to be up early tomorrow." She shrugged. "Farm life."

The Button women nodded in understanding.

"Hit me up online," George said as she climbed out of the truck and turned toward Brynn. "It'll be good to talk to someone my age."

"Tell me about it," Brynn huffed. "Between my dad and his friends, I spend most of my time hanging out with old people."

"Same," George said, then she turned to Willow and Lou and said, "Sorry, you two."

Lou and Willow laughed.

"I would've thought you meant Silas if you hadn't said that," Lou said with a groan. "Now I feel about one hundred."

George's cheeks turned red in the light from Brynn's porch. They said their goodbyes, urging Brynn once more to talk to her mother before returning to Lou's car.

With that, they drove back toward Button.

"Is it too late to go to Mrs. Kyle's house?" Lou asked. It had seemed perfectly reasonable going to the eccentric Francis's mansion at such an hour, but the woman who was their next questioning target also had to wake up early tomorrow for her job at the high school.

Willow waved a hand. "She's a night owl. We used to play *Words with Friends* all the time, and she and I were usually the last ones up, playing against each other when there wasn't anyone left."

So, Lou drove to the Forest Pond neighborhood, parking outside a cute white house with black trim and a tidy lawn. Willow ascended the porch steps first, followed closely by George, since Mrs. Kyle would be more likely to recognize them over Lou.

She opened the door after one ring of the doorbell, holding a pint-sized carton of ice cream in one hand and a television remote in the other.

"Oh, goodness," she said. "You've caught me." Looking down at the dessert, she added, "I was just in the middle of my guilty pleasure, the newest season of *The Bachelor*." She giggled. "I just love all the drama."

Willow grinned. "Well, what would you say to taking a break so we can fill you in on a little local drama?"

Mrs. Kyle stepped aside, a sparkle in her eyes as she said, "Come on in. Who wants some ice cream?"

While George said she'd take a bowl, Willow and Lou declined. They sat on her couch while she scooped George a serving. The woman was really into wolves. Lou noticed a wolf tapestry hanging on one wall, a wolf throw on the couch, and a watercolor painting of wolves running along a ridge in the kitchen.

"What's this all about?" Mrs. Kyle asked, handing George a bowl and spoon.

George dug in.

Willow sighed. "I need to know how Carly's doing in the new horticulture position."

Mrs. Kyle's face fell into a practiced customer service

smile. "Why, she's doing just wonderfully. The kids are loving her class, and—"

"Lonnel," Willow said the woman's first name in a low tone that sounded a lot like a warning.

Lou had never heard anyone call the woman by her first name.

Mrs. Kyle's cheeks turned red, and she dropped the act. Her expression fell into a frown. "It's terrible, dear. The woman's trying her best, but those kids are eating her alive. It's not just them either. The school board is talking about cutting her program."

Willow puffed out her cheeks. "I should've been paying closer attention. I should've left her with more specific lesson plans."

Placing her hand over Willow's, Mrs. Kyle clicked her tongue. "Nonsense. I saw what you left that woman." She addressed Lou and George as she said, "An entire two-year program outline with the different subjects and activities broken up into each semester and month." She focused on Willow once more. "You and I both know after working in education that some people have what it takes, and others don't, no matter how hard they try. They just don't have that spark, and kids can smell them a mile off."

"And maybe, if it's so bad that they're talking about cutting her program, Carly might've gotten desperate enough to take matters into her own hands?" Lou suggested.

George nodded, licking her spoon and placing it in the now-empty bowl. "Sometimes people who are desperate get delusional. If she thought Willow was the problem, maybe she thought getting rid of the cause would make her troubles go away too."

After such an inflammatory statement, they had to fill Mrs. Kyle in on their suspicions about the new horticulture teacher. None of them seemed to like the idea that Carly could've been pushed to where she was so desperate that she felt like she was out of options. But they also couldn't deny that she made sense as a suspect.

They thanked Mrs. Kyle and left her to the rest of her ice cream and show.

Once they were safely inside Lou's car, however, they sat in silence.

"So…" George said.

"So…" Willow repeated, seeming to be on the same page.

Lou gave voice to what they were all thinking. "Roy's never going to take his girlfriend's best friend seriously as a suspect, is he?"

George shook her head.

"That would be a hard no." Willow tapped her foot.

"And Easton's too good of a detective to do any investigating behind his coworker's back," Lou said. It wasn't a question. She knew they wouldn't be able to involve Easton. It could jeopardize not only his career but his reputation in the community.

"Which means we're looking into it together." George sounded way too excited about the prospect.

"Not tonight." Willow rubbed at her eyes. "I'm beat."

"Me too," Lou said. "Tomorrow, then." She drove them

each home, dreading what they would have to do the following day.

THE NEXT DAY WAS A MONDAY, so Lou considered closing the bookshop around lunch like she usually did, but after one and a half days closed that weekend, she could use the extra income, so she stayed open all day. Carly was still a teacher at the high school, so they wouldn't be able to question her at home until after school anyway. Lou had thought about showing up at the school on her lunch break to corner her but realized that would only make an already caged person feel even more attacked. No, it would be smarter to wait until she was in the safety of her own home.

Lou hoped they could reason with Carly.

The day went by in a blur. George came in along with Silas and Forrest in the morning, and the tulip tourists made Lou busy enough for the rest of the day that she barely had time to glance at the clock. Lou had also run out of cat food after feeding the cats lunch. She reminded herself to hit the pet store at some point that evening while she was out.

By the time she closed up and texted Willow that she was ready to leave, George was standing out in front of the bookstore, pacing.

"You okay?" Lou asked, exiting through the front door instead of the back like she normally did. She motioned for George to follow her around to her car.

George's gaze flicked up to meet Lou's and then away.

"It would be terrible to try to buy Geralt from Bella, right?" Her flighty eyes shifted to the ground. "She decorated a cake for him. There's no way she'll sell him," George muttered to herself, shaking her head.

Lou didn't seem to need to be a part of the conversation. George had already talked herself out of the plan. And as much as Lou understood the connection they'd had was amazing—and knowing how much it didn't seem like Bella cared for Buttons—she wasn't here to judge how people lived with their pets. He didn't appear to be in any danger of harm or neglect, so that was good. But if he'd run away once, he might do it again, and that was dangerous. He could get hit by a car, or the same coyote who'd probably found the poor ducklings' mother might get him.

Before they got into the car, Lou placed a hand on George's shoulder. "Maybe it'll help to see him in his home. It might give you closure."

George exhaled. "Maybe you're right."

Climbing into Lou's car, they headed for Willow's house to pick her up since she was on the way to Carly's home. Lou didn't even need to send Willow a text. She rushed out her front door the moment she saw Lou pull up.

"Someone's anxious," George muttered.

Lou shot her a sidelong glance. "Someone's supposed to be working in her nursery and has nothing better to do than worry."

George looked down at her hands in her lap. "Right."

Willow buckled herself into the back seat. "Okay, I'm ready. Did anyone think of a brilliant plan to explain why we're showing up at Carly's? Because all I've got is the fact that I think she might be a murderer, and I doubt that will win us any points in her favor."

Lou waited to back up, knowing Carly's home was just down the road and they wouldn't have much time to talk once she started driving.

"I thought maybe it could have to do with school." Lou turned in her seat so she could make eye contact with Willow. "Is there possibly something you forgot to share with her that you could suddenly remember and need to drop by to tell her?"

Willow pursed her lips. "I've emailed her a few times with those kinds of things, so it would be weird for me to suddenly show up to tell her this one in person."

George squared her shoulders. "I know." She turned to look at Lou and then Willow. "We don't go to Carly's. Why don't we go to Bella's? Maybe if I pretend that I really cannot live without Geralt and ask if I can buy him back, that'll give us a reason to be there."

It looked like George hadn't actually talked herself out of her earlier plan after all, Lou realized.

"Sure, pretending," Willow muttered.

George waved a hand dismissively. "All I'm saying is that it gets us in the door, so to speak. Then we can ask her about Carly and see if we can find out some information about where she was Friday night."

Lou nodded. "Okay, that's not a half-bad idea, actually. But are you willing to pay her for the cat if she really will sell it?"

"More than I probably should." George's eyes were filled with a heartbreaking amount of hope.

CHAPTER 19

For the second time in so many days, Lou pulled up to Bella Greene's house.

"What does she do again?" George asked in a hushed voice. "This is an enormous house."

Lou and Willow glanced at each other. They'd had dinner with the woman and yet could not, for the life of them, remember what she did.

"Ummm…" Willow cringed.

"Banking?" Lou guessed, knowing it was wrong, immediately.

George crossed her arms. "Well, whatever it is, she does it pretty darn well if she can afford a place like th—"

When George cut out, the two other women craned their necks to see what had gotten her attention. They didn't have to look far. Buttons, the cat, more recently known as Alexander Duclaw and Geralt, was picking his way around the barn. His gray coat was caked in mud and grime. He stopped midstep to shake out his whole body and lick at his paw before continuing on. George let out a squeak of protest as he slipped into the barn.

She opened the car door and went storming over. Lou and Willow raced after her.

Before George could reach the barn, however, someone called out, "What do you think you're doing?"

The three women froze, staring at the house. But the front door was still shut, and the porch was empty. Turning around, they found a woman standing in the middle of the circular driveway breathing heavily as if she'd just run over. That woman was Carly Zimmerman.

From the look of her car, parked haphazardly in the driveway behind them, lights still on, she'd raced over to stop what probably seemed like a break-in attempt at her best friend's home. To be honest, she wasn't that far off base.

Willow pasted on a smile. "Carly, it's so good to see you. I didn't know you lived here." Walking toward her, Willow pointed to the small green cottage that Lou had admired last time she was here.

But as Willow approached Carly, the replacement horticulture teacher ignored her predecessor, jogging around Willow and toward the barn. She put herself in between the red door and George, narrowing her eyes.

"I'll repeat my question. What are you doing here?" Carly asked. If Carly used the same tone with the high schoolers, she'd probably be able to get them to do any amount of homework, it was that terrifying.

George's shoulders slumped forward. "I miss Geralt." She waved a hand toward the barn. "Buttons. I convinced

Willow and Lou to bring me here to see if I could get Bella to consider selling him to me. I may have only had him for twenty-four hours, but we bonded. And I can't speak for him, but I don't think he's particularly fond of being an outdoor cat." She crossed her arms.

At that, Carly softened. She glanced back at the barn. "I've often thought the same thing." She looked right and left before whispering, "Bella doesn't even like cats. I don't know why she got him. She doesn't even really have a mouse problem for him to take care of. This barn is mostly for show."

Lou blinked at Carly's sudden candid streak. Willow and Lou were the kind of best friends who didn't tiptoe around the truth when it came to one another—and regularly called each other out on behavior they knew was counterproductive. But they wouldn't ever air that kind of dirty laundry to complete strangers.

"Why haven't you said something to her, then?" Willow asked, voicing the same thoughts Lou had just been thinking.

Carly pushed up the curtain of black bangs on her forehead so she could rest the heel of her hand there. "The only reason I can afford to rent that place is because of her." She hitched a thumb in the direction of the cute cottage. "And if you've met Bella, you know she doesn't exactly take criticism well."

Willow scoffed. "You can say that again."

"So the two of you aren't best friends?" Lou asked.

Carly's cheeks reddened, and she glanced down. "I wanted to be her friend, and at first it was really fun. But then I realized it was always about control with her and never about me." Carly's eyes flashed up to meet theirs, embarrassment deepening the color in her cheeks even more. "That sounds selfish. I don't need it to be *all* about me. I just want a friend who seems to care. Things haven't been so easy for me lately." At that comment, she locked eyes with Willow.

"What's been going on?" Lou asked, hoping to get her to open up, maybe even confess. As much compassion as Lou felt for Carly, she couldn't forget that the woman standing in front of her had been caught on camera stealing a branch off a very toxic tree that was used to kill a man the following day.

Carly shook out her hands and let them drop by her sides. "The kids, and parents, even the staff can't seem to shut up about the *amazing* Willow Grey." The way she said the word made it sound just the opposite. "I'm living in a constant shadow at work, and then I come home and I'm bombarded with Bella's issues. Because I'm renting from her, apparently that gives her the right to just come over whenever she wants." Carly paced.

Lou reached out and pulled George back toward her and Willow ever so slowly.

"It's too much for one person, you know? I can't hear about Bella's romantic obsessions anymore or watch her treat that poor man like he's nothing better than one of last season's handbags, and if I had to hear one more kid whisper something about how much more fun it was when Ms. Grey was there, I was going to snap." Carly's fingers clenched into fists.

Willow gulped. Lou glanced over at her car, trying to count the paces and plan how quickly they could make a run for it.

George cleared her throat. "You mean, you *did* snap. You snapped off a branch of that toxic tree."

Carly's eyes were rimmed with white. "I know it was trespassing, but I needed that branch. I had to win over those kids. And Kevin Schroeder had just gotten back from Key West with his family. He kept bragging about how he'd seen a deadly tree, and none of the kids believed him. I immediately knew which one he was talking about, and I'd even seen one just the other day when I was driving through Brine." She stared off into the sky as she said, "Bringing in something so dangerous had to get me some of the 'cool points' Willow had with the kids."

"Wait. The manchineel tree was to … show the kids?" Lou sputtered out the question.

It was as if Carly's monologue had been slowly filling up an enormous balloon labeled "guilty," and Lou's question popped it in one prick.

Her gaze turned dark. "Yeah, but even that backfired because one of the kids touched it even when I told him not to, and he had an awful reaction. His parents are threatening to sue the school. Principal Henning said she's not sure if the horticulture program can survive something like that."

"Not to mention how much danger you put those students in." Willow stepped forward, but Lou's arm flashed out to stop her.

Carly rubbed her neck. "Don't bother lecturing me. I've

already heard it from Flora, the school board, and the parents."

"You didn't use the branch for anything else?" Lou asked.

Carly frowned. "What do you mean?"

"It's just … there was a man killed with manchineel fruit the night after you stole it, not too far from here." George moved a rock around with the toe of her sneaker.

Carly gasped. "No way. I had nothing to do with that."

"But where did you put the branch you stole?" Lou asked.

Carly's eyes flicked around as if she were doing the calculations of where it had been and who'd had access to it. "I wrapped it in a garbage bag and put it in my trunk the first night, then I brought it to school. Then when I got it home, I didn't want anyone else to get hurt with it, and you're not supposed to burn them because the ash can be toxic as well, so I hid it in there." She gestured to the small shed next to her green cottage.

Tentatively, the group walked over to the shed. With shaking fingers, Carly opened up the door. Inside were some garden tools, a few bags of mulch, a potting station, and a lawn mower. But there was no branch.

"Dude, I think someone stole your toxic tree branch." George let out a low whistle.

"And whoever did used it to kill Harley Bramble in Willow's nursery," Lou added. Whirling on Carly, she asked, "Where were you on Friday?"

"I was here all evening. It was the day the kid got hurt,

and I didn't get home until close to seven as it was," Carly blurted out the alibi.

"Did anyone see you here?" George asked.

Carly nodded emphatically. "Roy." The word, though short, started out forceful and then became almost a whisper by the broken end. She looked down at her shoes. "He was on the porch waiting for Bella when I got home. I sat with him while we waited for her." Carly's lips pulled up into a smile. "He's so easy to talk to." She glanced up, color moving up into her cheeks once more in embarrassment. "When Bella didn't come home by ten, he left to go home and I went inside my place."

Lou narrowed her eyes, remembering something Carly had said in her ranting. She'd mentioned that she was sick of the way Bella treated "that poor man." She'd also said something about Bella's romantic obsessions. Lou was about to ask for clarification on those two subjects when Carly rubbed her hands up and down her arms.

"It's getting a little chilly out here. Do you mind if we talk inside?" Carly pointed to her cottage.

Though it had been in the sixties earlier, a dark cloud had moved in front of the sun, and the temperature had dropped considerably.

Willow checked with Lou and George before nodding. They waited for Carly to turn off her headlights and grab her stuff out of her car, which she'd exited earlier with so much haste, and then they followed her inside. Lou didn't miss the longing look George shot toward the barn as they went inside.

"Anyone thirsty?" Carly asked as she shrugged out of her jacket and toed off her boots.

"We're good," Lou answered for the lot of them. Carly may not be the murderer, but she still wasn't feeling trusting toward the woman just yet. There still seemed to be something she was hiding.

"Okay, I'm just going to grab some water. Make yourselves at home," Carly called from the kitchen.

The three women perched on the cream-colored sofa in the cozy living room.

"You have really great design sense," Lou commented. "The decorations in this place are adorable."

Carly walked back into the room, holding a glass of water. "Oh, it was fully furnished when I got here. Bella hired a decorator."

"Okay, what does Bella do?" George asked, blurting out the question before either of the older women had a chance to remind her it wasn't an especially polite thing to ask.

Smiling, Carly said, "It took me a long time to figure that out too." She giggled. "The answer is, pretty much nothing. Her family is super rich. I think she's technically the 'something' of operations for the business, but she seems to have a lot of time on her hands for a business mogul. She even hires someone to gather the eggs from those chickens she brags about."

"Rich family." George nodded slowly, as if that all made sense now.

"Oh, right." Willow snapped her fingers. "She said that during dinner."

Lou remembered now, too, but she was more interested in something else Carly had said. "You mentioned something about how Bella treats Roy. Does she not actually like him?" As annoying as the detective could be, Lou felt defensive of him.

Carly rolled her eyes. "She's super hot and cold with the poor guy. One minute, she's all over him, the next she's standing him up, and he's stuck talking to me on the porch for hours. All I know is that she doesn't actually like Roy."

That was news to Lou and Willow, who'd seen firsthand how disgustingly affectionate Bella and Roy were during their dinner together.

"Then why is she dating him?" George asked.

Again, Carly's attention locked on to Willow. "To get closer to the guy she really likes, the one she's been obsessed with her whole life."

Lou had a bad feeling about what was coming next.

George must've, too, because she grimaced and leaned back.

"She's obsessed with Easton, always has been," Carly told Willow. "And she told me the other day that she'd do anything to break the two of you up."

CHAPTER 20

A full-body shiver racked Lou's body at Carly's comment.

"Anything?" Willow asked, the word breathy with realization.

George leaned forward. "Wait. On Friday, when Bella stood up Roy, did you see what time she finally got home?"

The question proved to Lou that she wasn't alone in her line of thinking.

Carly shrugged. "I have no idea. I went to bed. It was late, and I'd had such a long day." She looked from George to Lou to Willow. Her facial expression descended deeper into a frown with each movement. "Omigosh, you think she was the one to kill that man at Willow's nursery?"

Willow paled. "Maybe she thought that making it seem like I was a murderer might break up Easton and me."

"And Martie, the Ryde driver who gave the killer a ride afterward, said it was too dark to tell who the person was, especially because they didn't talk. It could've been a woman with her hair tucked into a beanie in that car with Harley's phone." George snapped her fingers, obviously having heard the same town gossip that they had.

It was then that Lou was reminded exactly *who* had told them about the Ryde the killer called to take them away from the crime scene. Bella. All Lou could seem to recall in the following seconds was the smug way she talked, in detail, about how it had all gone down, about how *smart* it was of the killer to use Harley's phone to order the getaway car and then leave his phone in the car so they wouldn't have to worry about getting rid of the evidence.

At the time, Lou had thought of it as merely gossip Bella was sharing, but what if it was some sick game to see how much she could tell them about a crime she'd committed in front of two detectives?

Lou jabbed a thumb behind them, toward the shed they'd just looked inside minutes ago. "The manchineel branch is missing. Bella could've seen you put it there and snuck over the following night to take it."

Carly's lips parted in surprise, but she didn't refute any of the claims they were making. It was all possible.

Except one thing.

"How would she know about the toxicity of the manchineel tree, though?" Lou thought aloud. "Did you talk to her about it?"

"I didn't need to. Her family is the Greenes," Carly said.

Lou stared blankly at the woman. George tilted her head as if waiting for more.

Willow frowned. "Yeah, we know her last name. What does that mean?"

"They own Northwest Plants," Carly explained.

Lou's whole body prickled with an intense mixture of fear and excitement. That was it, the last piece of the puzzle. Now that it was complete, it created a terrible picture of a jealous person who'd gone to horrible lengths to try to get something they thought they deserved.

"She did it," Willow whispered.

Carly opened her mouth again. This time it seemed like words would actually come out, but George interrupted her.

"There's no way Roy is going to believe his girlfriend is the killer." George cut the air with her palm.

Lou was inclined to agree. "We need more evidence."

"What more does he need?" Willow scoffed. "Plus, I'm sure we could show him a picture of her stuffing that fruit into Harley's mouth, and he would still deny she had any part in this."

"We need a confession," Lou said, resolute. "Preferably on video."

Excitement burst from George as she said, "We can trap her. Maybe we hide and get good ole Carly here to pull the information out of her, all while we're somewhere close by getting it all on video."

"It wouldn't be admissible in court." Willow shook her head.

"But it could be enough to convince Roy to gather actual evidence against her," George countered.

Willow pressed her lips together, considering the idea.

Before she could agree to the plan or not, Carly's front door opened. Bella Greene strode inside.

"What's going on here?" The way she asked was so forceful yet edged with a sweetness that was faker than aspartame. It made Lou want to shrink back into the corner of the room, far away from the killer.

George stood up, and Lou just about leapt forward to tackle her back to the ground. But then George said, "Bella, I'm here to buy your cat."

Lou relaxed and let it play out. George had a plan.

"I know I only had him for a day, but I fell in love with him," George explained. "I know outdoor cats can have a great life, too, but I really don't think he's suited for that kind of life. He looks miserable. I came to offer you money for him, but you weren't home, so we talked to Carly while we waited."

"About school stuff," Carly blurted unhelpfully. She motioned to Willow. "Since Willow used to have my job."

Lou inwardly cursed the woman's poor acting skills. But now was not the time to give Carly improv pointers. She turned her focus on Bella, studying the woman as she took it all in. Her sharp eyes scanned the room, narrowing every so often as if she were a robot and wanted to zoom in on certain things that she found suspicious.

The quiet padding of mice feet would've sounded like elephant footsteps in the silent room as everyone waited on Bella's answer. No one dared breathe, let alone move.

Bella pushed back her shoulders. From the smirk that curled over her lips, she was enjoying the attention. Bella looked George up and down, then glared at Willow.

Finally, she said, "No."

Just like that. George crumpled back onto the couch in defeat.

Willow stood. "You don't even like him." She jabbed an accusing finger at the woman. "This isn't about George or the cat. Admit it. This is about me."

"Fine." Bella arched an eyebrow. "It is." She shot a quick scowl in Carly's direction, as if she knew Carly had spilled her secret.

"And you think denying a poor animal a home where someone actually likes him and wants him is going to break up me and Easton?" Willow shifted her stance as if she needed to be ready to jump out of Bella's way if she came racing toward her.

Bella shrugged. "No, getting to deny your friend something she wants is just a bonus. But I do think Easton seeing what a mess you are might do the trick." Bella ticked the reasons off on her fingers. "Can't keep your pets straight, quit your steady job for some silly dream, can't even seem to open the dream nursery, and now you're the suspect in a murder investigation." She clicked her tongue. "Easton is a classy guy. He's a good detective with a great reputation. You are only dragging down his status with the locals, making him into a laughingstock."

Lou's heart hurt for her friend. Even though none of the terrible things Bella was saying were true, Lou knew Willow had insecurities just like everyone. And sometimes hearing them voiced outside of your destructive inner monologue could be jarring. She was about to stand up and tell Bella just how wrong she was, but Willow beat her to it.

"You're so sad." Willow let out a humorless chuckle.

"Whether I'm good enough to be with Easton is something I want to hear only from Easton. And, honestly, if I thought any of that would sway him from wanting to be with me, *I* wouldn't want to be with *him*. But that's not the case. Easton isn't going anywhere, certainly not to you."

Lou felt like clapping. Movement next to her caught her eye, and she noticed George had slipped her phone out of her pocket and was starting a video recording. Over the arm of the couch, the camera just barely caught Bella's face. Bella glanced in that direction, but Lou chose that moment to jump up and give in to the clapping.

"Well said, Willow." Lou glared at Bella, successfully pulling her attention away from George and her camera.

As if buoyed by her friend's support, Willow kept going. "And, if you think me being a suspect in a murder investigation is going to make Easton not want to be with me anymore, what do you think it's going to do to his opinion of you when he finds out you're the actual murderer?"

It seemed as though all the blood left Lou's body at once. Or maybe that was just any warmth in the room being sucked right out the door. The chill that Bella's rage emitted throughout the space was a cold fog.

Oh no, Lou thought. *Willow was on a roll, but she took it too far. And now we're in a room with a murderer who knows we know she's a murderer.*

Lou gently grabbed on to Willow's arm, wishing she hadn't just said that. But she had, and they might need to run.

But instead of cackling like a villain who's been caught, or smirking in delight that someone figured out the truth,

Bella coughed in surprise. "Murderer? What do you mean?"

Willow's previous confidence waned as she doubted the truth of the statements she'd just hurled at Bella like weapons.

"You killed Harley Bramble in my nursery, so I would be the prime suspect. You stole Steve to make me appear incompetent." Willow's tone was edged with hysteria, like she wasn't sure what it would mean if those things weren't true.

Bella shook her head. "Wrong yet again." She shot Willow a pitying look, as if it were the saddest thing she'd ever witnessed.

But just as Lou was questioning everything, Carly stepped forward, pointing a finger toward Bella. "She's lying, and I can prove it."

CHAPTER 21

Bella's eye twitched as she glared at her tenant. "Carly," she said in a low warning. "Think about this for a moment."

There was so much unspoken behind that sentence. Carly's gaze flicked around the room as she seemed to do just that. Bella controlled her housing. She could kick her out at a moment's notice—would, if the menacing look she was shooting Carly's way was any indication.

But Carly shook her head. "I can't keep your secrets anymore. Kick me out. I don't care. Living next to you is awful anyway. You come over *whenever* you feel like it, without even knocking. And you're not a good friend. Friendship goes both ways. It's a give and take." Carly waved a hand toward Lou and Willow.

It was a gesture that might've warmed Lou's heart in less intense circumstances. As it was, Lou was becoming increasingly worried about Carly's safety. If Carly was right, and Bella was lying about not being the murderer, then Carly had bigger things to worry about than being evicted.

The words Carly threw at Bella didn't even seem to sting, making Lou sure the woman was even more heartless than she'd first imagined. If anything, the words just made Bella mad.

She took a step forward. "I don't know what you're talking about." Her eye twitched as she held the woman's gaze.

Carly stepped back. "You have Willow's goat in the barn." She pointed out to the red-and-white barn where Buttons, the cat, had disappeared earlier. "I saw him the other day."

George gasped. "That's why you stopped us from going in there! But why wouldn't you want us to find him if you knew she had him?"

"I thought I could talk her into putting him back at night so Willow wouldn't know it was her." Carly's shoulders sank forward. "I was still trying to protect her." She swallowed and stood up straight. "But that's before I knew the truth, before I knew you wouldn't stop at kidnapping someone's pet."

Bella's expression flashed with anger. "What's that supposed to mean?"

"The tree limb I had in that plastic bag in the shed is gone." Carly hitched a thumb toward the shed in the front yard. "That's what was used to kill that poor auditor." Tears flooded Carly's eyes. "You can't lie to us anymore. We know the truth. I sat with Roy while he waited for you that night. You stood him up because you took that branch and used it to kill that auditor on Willow's property."

A laugh bubbled out of Bella. At first, it seemed like the maniacal cackle of a murderer. But after a few moments, it morphed into the uncontrollable giggle of someone who's been told a silly joke that's so absurd that they can't believe they still find it funny.

Carly's watery eyes narrowed into a frown, and she looked from Bella to Lou, Willow, and George in confusion.

Wiping at her eyes, Bella controlled her cackling and sighed. "It's just funny how wrong you are."

"Don't do that," Carly warned, now her turn to use the low, commanding tone. "I've seen the goat. He's out in the barn right now. I can show them."

Bella raised her eyebrows in challenge. "Fine. Go for it. You won't find him out there."

"Why? What did you do to him?" Willow tried to walk forward, but Lou was already grasping her arm and holding her back.

"Bella, you've already lied to us multiple times tonight. Why would we believe you now?" Lou asked, trying to reason with her instead of resorting to a physical confrontation.

"Yeah," George chimed in. "You were gone during the evening when the auditor was killed, had access to the manchineel tree branch that's now missing, work for a company that the auditor was giving a hard time to, and threatening to hit with fees and citations, and you also had the underlying bonus of messing with Willow's life. It all makes sense to me."

Bella frowned. "What about my family's business?"

"We, uh, may have come across some evidence that Harley Bramble gave Northwest Plants a rather large citation. It was later taken care of. Was that through bribery or just plain threats?" Lou asked.

Willow nodded. "Yeah, because we've seen the stock your family sold to the garden center in Brine. It definitely had verticillium wilt, and yet the fines just went away?"

Bella cut the air with her palm. "My family's business had nothing to do with that man's death, and neither did I. Yes, I took that tree branch, but I brought it to my family's corporate office in Kirk and disposed of it in our big trash compactor so no one would get hurt. I just wish I'd done that before Carly took it to school and that silly kid touched it." She rolled her eyes. "I didn't kill Harley Bramble, and neither did anyone at my family's company," she repeated, like she was repeating her thesis at the end of a term paper.

"And the goat?" Carly asked.

"Fine," Bella said with a bored sigh. "I took Willow's goat, but I just put him back this evening. That's why he's not in the barn."

Like a sailboat that had been coasting along and suddenly lost its wind, the three women stood there, not sure where to go now.

"You took Steve, but you swear you had nothing to do with Harley Bramble's murder?" Lou wasn't sure why she needed to hear it again, but she still wasn't convinced.

"I went to Kirk that evening with the toxic tree branch," Bella explained. "While I was there, I got to talking to my family. We ended up going out to dinner together. I'm sure there are receipts, and the server could probably tell you we were all there and accounted for. That's how I know they're all innocent too."

"Do you even care that you stood up Roy that evening?" Carly asked.

"Not really." Bella squinted one eye. "I was just with him to get closer to Easton anyway."

"That's why you wanted to go on a double date with us." Willow let out a disappointed chuckle.

She smiled, happy to take credit for that.

"Well, if you don't care about Roy, you'll be fine telling him all about your alibi and letting him check it, right?" Lou pushed.

Bella nodded. "Sure. Whatever. If you insist."

"We do." George stood, finally ending the recording. She shook her phone at the woman. "And don't backpedal once we're around him. I've got the whole thing on video."

A muscle jumped in Bella's jaw. "You are all *so* intense. Do you know that?"

"We can live with being intense." Lou motioned to the door. "Come on. We're going to see Roy right now. Carly, can you come with us?"

Carly started for her jacket. "I'd be happy to."

Willow hesitated. "Do you mind if I don't go?" she asked, her eyes pleading with Lou. "I'd love it if you could drop me off at home so I can see Steve."

"Of course," Lou said with a smile. "We'll take care of Bella's story."

And with that, the odd group piled into Lou's car and drove to the police station, stopping to let Willow out at home on the way by.

It was a good thing George had taken the video because even though Bella told the truth once they got to the station, Roy wouldn't believe her until he watched the whole conversation.

He flinched at the times Bella mentioned him and how she'd been using him, and it seemed those comments really pushed him over the edge and helped him see the truth. As much sympathy as Lou had for the man, she had a feeling he'd be okay, especially if the looks Carly and he shared were any sign. He seemed to appreciate the times Carly had stood up for him and said he was a good man.

Once he accepted Bella was telling the truth, he'd been able to confirm her alibi, as well as noting that her mother, father, and brother were all at the dinner with her—thanks to the security system at the gas station across the street from the restaurant.

As much relief as Lou was filled with upon her exit from the police station, there was an equal amount of concern because if Bella and Carly were both cleared for the murder of Harley Bramble, who'd committed the crime? And if it wasn't a personal vendetta against Willow, why had the crime taken place at Willow's nursery?

"You're right about Buttons," Bella said as they left the station together. She shrugged at George. "He hates being an outdoor cat, and I don't like him enough to let him come inside. He's yours."

George's eyes went wide. "Are you sure?"

Bella nodded. "If you want to come pick him up now, you're more than welcome to."

Lou smiled, detaching her car key from her ring and putting it in George's palm. "Take my car. Go get him. I'll walk home."

George hugged Lou and squealed as she and Bella climbed into Lou's car.

It was closing in on nine as Lou walked the two blocks back to the bookshop. She was excited for a nice relaxing night at home. But that was all shot out the window the moment she stepped foot inside.

"Cat food." She groaned. She'd forgotten to grab some while she was out.

The hungry faces of Sapphire, Anne Mice, Catnip Everdeen, and Charles Lickens caused a swell of guilt inside her heart. Normally, she would've just walked down the street to the pet store to grab their food. But it was late and it would already be closed. The only places that were open this late, in fact, were the big-box stores over in Kirk.

"I'll be back in a bit, kittens," she assured them, but stopped short as she remembered George had her car. "Right." She kicked the toe of her shoe against the floor.

She didn't want to rush George, and she wasn't about to pull Willow away from Steve this soon after she'd just gotten him back. That was when it hit her. Ryde! Button now had its first Ryde driver. She pulled up the app and entered a new Ryde destination, waiting to see whether Martie would pick it up, which she did almost immediately, and Lou exhaled in relief. She sent off a quick text to George.

> Hold on to the car tonight. I'll come grab it and the keys in the morning.

George texted back a thumbs-up and a celebration emoji. Lou guessed picking up Geralt was going well.

Martie's minivan pulled up in front of the bookstore a few minutes later. Lou hopped inside, enjoying the lavender scent of the interior and the snacks in a basket in between the two middle seats.

"Welcome to my Ryde," Martie said, her scratchy voice sounding uncharacteristically pleasant. "Sit back and enjoy the trip."

Lou buckled in. "Thanks, Martie. I just needed some cat food, and Kirk's the closest place at this time of night. George has my car."

"Ah, no problem. We'll get those little fostered felines of yours some food." Martie chuckled and started toward the larger city to the south.

"How's your dad doing?" Lou asked.

Silas talked about him every so often. Button House had a more independent living section, where Silas lived in an apartment, but it also housed much more medically dependent patients like Martie's father in the other wing.

Martie smiled at her in the rearview mirror. "Oh, he's

doing okay. Good days and bad. Thank you for asking. A bugger of a disease, Alzheimer's."

"I'm so sorry. That must be so difficult." Lou shifted her weight in the seat. "Hey, Martie. You don't happen to…" Lou paused, not sure exactly how to word the rest of that sentence. She didn't want to seem like she was prying, but really, that *was* what she wanted to do.

"Remember anything about the killer that night?" Martie finished for her.

Lou exhaled a chuckle. "Yeah. Sorry. You must be getting that question a lot."

Martie shrugged as she took a turn. "I don't mind. It's really not all that glamorous. I *wish* I remembered more, but there were just a couple of things."

Lou wished she wasn't wearing a seatbelt, so she could lean closer to Martie.

"They were wearing a hoodie, pulled up over their head, wore a mask and sunglasses so I couldn't see their face," Martie explained. "Thought they were just sick or something; though, I was a little scared that they might try to rob me, but with a name like Harley Bramble, I figured they couldn't be that bad." Martie barked out a laugh. "The other thing was that the person kept clearing their throat. It was really annoying." Martie imitated the sound. "And they smelled like cinnamon gum."

Lou sat back in defeat. Everyone cleared their throats. That wasn't anything that could help them catch a killer. And the gum made sense, given the folded wrappers she'd found on the scene, but again, it wasn't something unique they could use since many people chewed cinnamon gum.

It was probably the same conclusion Roy had reached when he'd undoubtedly questioned Martie.

Sitting back, Lou resigned herself to just enjoying the trip out to Kirk to get the cat food. She turned the conversation toward the tulip tourists, and Martie entertained her the rest of the ride with tales of the funny things she'd encountered that week.

CHAPTER 22

The next day, Lou got a phone call from Willow about fifteen minutes before the bookshop was set to open.

"Good morning," Lou said, hopeful that the call she was receiving was of the positive variety and not the other way around.

"I got the all clear to reopen the nursery from Roy." Willow's tone was flat as if she were in shock.

A big smile pulled across Lou's face. "That's amazing, Willow. Are you going to open up today?"

Willow sighed. "I still have to wait for that new auditor to sign off on my stock, but he said he could come by this evening and run a portable version of the test."

"Right." Lou had almost forgotten meeting David, the new Harley, the day they'd found Harley's body. "Do you want me to come with you?"

"Maybe." The word was small.

Lou hated that Willow's nursery, a place she was so

enamored with before, was now a source of unease for her. But she remembered when she'd found that man dead behind her bookshop on her second day in town. It had been scary at first, but she'd eventually learned to feel comfortable in the space alone again. Some things just took time.

Knowing the truth behind what had happened to him had definitely helped, so Lou hoped Roy was at less of a stalemate with his guesses about who could've killed Harley than they were. Lou had shared Tessa Delaney's name with Roy yesterday before they'd left the station as a person of interest.

She'd convinced him to look up Tessa's government picture, and when she'd shown up as a woman with dark bluntly-cut hair, Lou told him about the woman she'd seen waiting in her car outside the nursery while the police had been working through the crime scene the day of the murder. She wasn't sure, since that woman had been wearing sunglasses and driving a very fancy car, but it could've been Tessa, checking up on the scene of the crime. Roy had promised to check into her though he wasn't sure if the motive was enough.

"If everyone went around killing people who wanted their jobs, we'd have very few people left in the world," Roy had said last night. But he'd also listened to her, which was more than she could usually say of the detective. She'd decided not to push it too much.

He was right. Tessa Delaney seemed like she had the weakest motive of anyone to get rid of Harley. The problem was, she was also the last person Lou could think of.

"Then I'll be there," Lou told Willow on the phone call. "I'll come over right after I close the shop, and we can head to the nursery. We can water the plants and make sure everything's looking good while we wait for David."

"Thanks, Lou." Willow's voice sounded settled, less tense than it had before. The bleat of a goat sounded in the background.

"Hi, Steve!" Lou called through the phone, giggling. "How's he doing?"

"Great," Willow said. "He's so happy to be back that he hasn't even slipped into the garden once. Okay, I'll see you this evening."

"Bye." Lou ended the call and focused on her morning tasks.

The rest of the day went by quickly. George came by with Geralt in his *cat carrier*, as she was calling it now. The moment anyone gave her guff for it, she would simply tell them she'd already been separated from him once, and she didn't want that to happen again.

After she closed up the bookshop, Lou walked over to George's house to grab her car. Following the directions on the sign next to the front door, she walked right inside.

"Welcome to the Technology Emporium," George's voice spilled out from a back room. "I'll be with you in a moment."

Someone else sat in George's regular recliner, fingers clicking over the buttons on a game controller. It was Brynn.

"It's just Lou," Brynn called over her shoulder to George and then smiled at Lou. "Hey."

Lou beamed. "Hey, good to see you again." She stepped farther into the house, feeling odd hanging out by the door.

Brynn paused the game and set down the controller. "George told me all about what happened last night. Wild stuff."

Laughing, Lou said, "That feels like an accurate description." Lou might also add terrifying, confusing, and surprising to the list. "You two hanging out?" She peered into the back room, looking for signs of George.

Brynn nodded. "She's off doing one last search through Harley's emails. Can't seem to let it go."

Sounds like me, Lou thought. She'd found her thoughts drifting to the case more than a few times that day.

"I didn't help, though," Brynn admitted. "I was telling her that I talked to my dad about all of this, and he told me he actually had to go through Northwest Plants to buy the manchineel tree. He said no other small buyers would get it for him since it's not supposed to be transported across state lines, and they could've gotten a big fine if they were caught with it."

Lou frowned. "But Northwest Plants is immune to such rules?" That didn't sit right with Lou. Big corporations shouldn't be able to get away with things small businesses weren't allowed to do.

Brynn quickly quashed her need for altruistic frustration, saying, "No, they're not allowed to, either, but Dad said they have a person on the inside of the state agriculture department who they were paying to illegally transport it for them. Apparently, he goes to the Caribbean for vacation all the time, so no one would know anything was up."

"He?" Lou asked, frowning. That threw her Tessa Delaney theory out the window. She was their only remaining suspect involved in the department, but if Northwest Plants was working with a man, that cut her out. "Do you think it could've been Harley? Was he their inside man?"

"And he died from the very plant he'd just transported up here?" Brynn pursed her lips. "I don't know. It doesn't sound likely."

"What if he betrayed their confidence, and he was going to turn them in or report them or something?" Excitement built in Lou. The fact that Northwest Plants had gotten off without a citation when they'd obviously had the disease present in their stock spoke to other ways in which Harley could've been giving them breaks and inside deals. "The Northwest Plants execs were all out to dinner that evening, but isn't that odd?"

Brynn shrugged like she guessed so but wasn't making the connections Lou was.

"Bella said her mom just sprang the dinner on her while she was visiting the office. Was it to give the whole family alibis because they knew what was about to happen?" Lou was pacing now. "Of course, really rich people wouldn't do the killing themselves. I'm sure they hired a hit man or something," she scoffed, unsure why she hadn't seen it before.

Last night had been such a blur, but she definitely remembered Carly mentioning that Bella even hired someone to gather her eggs from the chickens she insisted on having. If she couldn't even do that, of course, her corrupt family wouldn't do their own killing. And what if the woman with the dark hair and glasses in the expensive car that morning hadn't been Tessa Delaney, but Mrs. Greene, there to check that her hit man had done the job?

"I've got to go," Lou said, waving to Brynn. "Say hi to George for me and tell her I got my keys." She grabbed them from the table in the corner, waving them in the air so Brynn saw she had them.

Once in her car, Lou sent a quick text to Willow.

> On my way. Just making one quick stop at the station to see Roy.

Willow sent a thumbs-up and then an intrigued emoji.

Lou would explain everything once she got there. First, she needed to see what the lead detective on the case thought.

"A CONNECTION with Northwest Plants is definitely a better guess than your last one," Detective Roy Anderson said as he narrowed his eyes at Lou. "Is this the woman you saw that morning?" He turned his computer monitor until it faced Lou.

The woman on the screen was an exact match to the one she'd seen waiting in the car that day.

"That's her," Lou said. Finally, something was clicking. She was almost breathless after having raced through the explanation of why she thought Harley had been working behind the scenes for Northwest Plants and had made them mad, so they got rid of him, using the very plant he'd just smuggled into town for them.

Roy jotted down a few notes. "I'll bring in Jeremiah Pine to verify exactly what the Northwest Plants exec told him, and see if he'll spill who it was." Roy eyed Lou. "Do you think he'll cooperate this time? Last visit I made out to his farm wasn't exactly a warm or talkative one."

Lou nodded. She would send Brynn and George a message to prep Jeremiah, tell him that he had to tell the truth because it might mean justice in a murder. "I'll make sure he talks to you." Lou recalled what Brynn had said about the downsides of small towns. "But maybe invite him to come here and talk to you instead of showing up on his farm this time. He'll probably take that a lot better."

"I can do that." Roy added to his note. "After that, I'll see if I can verify any of this about Mr. Bramble. It should be fairly easy to see if he'd taken any recent vacations." At that, Roy stood. "Thanks for coming in."

Lou felt a surge of hope inside her heart. He was taking her seriously again. This was some kind of record. She glanced at him. He looked a little tired after last night.

"I'm sorry about Bella," she added before she followed him.

His dark eyes met hers. At first, they flashed with anger in a *How dare you?* kind of threat, but that quickly simmered into disappointment. "Thanks. I guess I should've known. Already did, if I'm being really honest with myself." He rubbed the back of his neck.

"But Carly seems interested," Lou added. "Maybe you should call her."

A smile curled at the corner of Roy's mouth. "I might just do that. Thanks, Lou."

Waving, Lou left Detective Anderson to his research, and hopefully to finally wrap up this case. She shot a quick text over to George, telling her to have Brynn prep her dad for the call he was about to receive from the detective. George sent back a thumbs-up, and Lou headed to Willow's.

Willow and Easton sat on the front porch when Lou pulled up. They waved as she got out, coming to say hello.

"Hear you stopped by to talk to Roy," Easton said as she approached.

"And I think he actually listened." Lou turned to Willow. "Not only that, but I think we may have solved who killed Harley." She explained exactly what she'd learned from Brynn and how it had triggered the solution in her mind. "Roy's checking into it all, but he seemed convinced too."

"So Bella might've been involved after all?" Willow asked.

Lou shook her head. "I think she's just as out of the loop about any illegal activity as she is about anything that goes on at her family business. Her mother probably just invited her to make it look even better that they were having dinner all together."

Easton blinked. "That sounds about right. It's my day off, but maybe I'll go in and help Roy get some of those statements. And he may need backup if he's going to have to bring in big company executives. You two have a good time at the nursery. Let me know how the soil test goes." Easton stood, kissing Willow before heading for his house.

But before he could even leave the porch, a shiny black SUV pulled in next to Lou in Willow's driveway. Bella Greene spilled out, looking like a mess of a person. Her dark hair was in a matted bun on her head, as if she'd slept in it and hadn't run a comb through it in days. She wore one shoe, but the other wasn't hooked around her heel. And her jacket dragged behind her as she raced out of her vehicle.

"Bella, what's this about?" Easton's tone was as steely as his gray eyes. He'd heard all about her antics last night and had lowered his opinion of her even more.

Lou gulped, wondering if Bella had heard about her family and their possible involvement in Harley's death.

But Bella grimaced at Easton and then Willow, saying, "Can I talk to you two? I just have a few things to say, starting with how sorry I am."

Easton and Willow shared a long look, but then Willow nodded.

Checking her watch, Lou said, "How about I meet you there? That way, you don't have to rush."

"That would be great. Thanks, Lou." Willow smiled. "Easton can drop me off in a few."

Waving, and leaving the three of them to their conversation, Lou drove to the nursery, glad she wasn't in Bella's shoes as she took one last look over her shoulder and caught a glimpse of the scowls Willow and Easton wore as they listened.

CHAPTER 23

Lou stood next to ValNur as she waited for David Houston to show up. She glanced up at the wooden troll with interest.

"You know what? You kind of grow on a person, ValNur," she told him, jumping as a car door slammed.

A car had pulled into the lot, and David stepped out holding a bag of testing supplies and a clipboard similar to the one they had found near Harley. Lou hoped he hadn't seen her talking to the troll just then.

"Hi," she said, walking forward to meet him.

"No Willow today?" he asked.

Lou waved a hand. "I told her I'd handle this." Lou wasn't sure how long Bella's talk would take, so she didn't want to make promises about Willow showing up when she might be detained longer. "Come on. I'll let you inside."

He laughed. "I don't know what Harley was talking about. He had such a hard time with her, but if she's anything like you, I'm sure I'll find her perfectly pleasant."

Lou hoped he would be able to see the good in Willow, especially if he'd be taking over the Lakeside County duties. "She was pretty stressed out the week he came out. She's usually not like that. He told you about it?"

David flinched. "Well, we've got an email chain for the different county auditors. Mostly it's a place to share information that might be pertinent from one county to the next, but sometimes it's also nice to vent about interesting encounters we have on the job."

Having a much less favorable view of Harley after learning he was probably taking bribes to look the other way as a corporation broke the law, Lou kept her mouth shut, figuring the less she said, the better. She unlocked the new deadbolt Willow and Peggy Lee had purchased for the place and led him inside.

"Okaaay," she said, realizing she didn't know what she was supposed to do next. Turning to him, she whispered, "What do we do now?" even though they were the only two people there.

David cleared his throat. "*You* don't have to do anything. I've got it from here." He hitched the bag of supplies he carried a little higher and patted the side of it. "Basically, I'm going to walk around testing soil from the different plants to make sure there isn't any evidence of *the wilt*." He wiggled his fingers as if it were the monster in a Halloween horror story.

Lou hoped there wouldn't be. Willow really didn't need another setback.

As if he sensed Lou's trepidation, David leaned in close,

clearing his throat again before he whispered, "Don't worry. Everything looks exceptionally healthy. Again, I'm actually not sure what Harley was going on about. It must've been more about her unwillingness to cooperate than him being worried her stock was carrying verticillium wilt or root rot."

That settled the majority of Lou's fears. "Great," she said. "I guess I'll be around if you need anything. I'll probably just be doing some watering."

He gave her a salute and wandered over to the nearest bench of plants and opened his bag. Leaning over to dig around inside, his shirt collar moved down, displaying a rather impressive tan line along his neck, like where a T-shirt might cover while someone was sitting on the beach.

Lou grabbed the nearest hose, turning on the water and mindlessly soaking the plants. Willow's warnings about the hoses tripping customers and avoiding the blast setting on the nozzle repeated in Lou's mind while she let her thoughts follow whatever it was latching on to about that tan line. That was right. Harley had supposedly just come back from a Caribbean vacation, where he'd smuggled in the manchineel tree for Jeremiah, but the man was as pale as a sheet from what Lou remembered of that day they found his body.

She moved on to the next section of plants. He was dead when she saw him, and had been all night. Of course, he would be paler than he had been while living.

But David seemed to have fresh tan lines. And even though the sun had been making more appearances lately as the Pacific Northwest moved into spring, his tan seemed much too intense to have been procured by sitting out in this sunshine.

Then there was the throat clearing. Martie had said the person in her car had done it a few times. David had definitely cleared his throat more than usual in the short time she'd talked to him. And had that been a hint of cinnamon on his breath when he'd leaned in close to talk to her? Or was her mind playing tricks on her?

The hairs on Lou's arm stood on end. What if they'd been wrong about which auditor was in the pocket of Northwest Plants? She turned to get another look at David, only to realize he was gone.

Lou dropped the hose, glancing over her shoulder as she skirted toward the closest greenhouse, hoping for a little cover. Peeking inside, she didn't see David anywhere. She dashed to the middle opening that served as the main walkway through the nursery. That was when she caught sight of him. He was just inside the gate, standing in front of Willow's office, the tiny house that had once belonged to another local. He pulled a folded piece of paper from his pocket. A chain of gum wrappers came out with the paper. The chain fell to the ground with a metallic flutter. Unaware of what he'd dropped, yet again, David slipped the paper under Willow's office door.

Ducking behind the plastic greenhouse wall as David checked over his shoulder, Lou's heart hammered in her chest. She wasn't sure what he'd slipped under the door, but she definitely recognized the gum wrapper chain that had fallen out of his pocket. It was just like the one that had been near Harley's body.

What if David's gum of choice was cinnamon, and he collected the wrappers to make into the chains to keep his fingers busy when he was stressing about the illegal things he was doing for Northwest Plants?

It hit Lou that if Harley had complained about Willow on their auditor email thread, only another auditor would know Willow would be a good scapegoat for the crime.

Lou moved as quickly and quietly as she could toward the back of the nursery. She wanted to put as much space between David and herself as possible. Once she was standing near the back corner, she pulled out her phone. There were no texts or calls from Willow, nothing to make her think she was on her way. Lou started a new text.

> Are you on your way? Can you bring Easton? David is acting sketchy and

"I'm going to need you to hand that over." David's voice interrupted what Lou was typing.

She jumped, startled by his presence. Her fingers froze above the screen as she turned around. David's once amenable smile now looked like the evil smirk of a madman. Lou's blood seemed to freeze in her veins as the flash of metal by his side proved to her that there would be recourse if she didn't give him her phone. After all she'd heard about the manchineel tree, it sounded terrifying, but a gun still scared her more.

Swallowing, Lou said, "You were the one working with Northwest Plants. You brought the tree back from the Caribbean and … what, did Harley catch you?"

David's expression tightened. "I tried to cut him in on

the deal, but the guy was too focused on being the boss, one day. He didn't want anything on his record that could put that in jeopardy. When he told us he was coming to meet with Willow one more time, that he'd finally gotten her to consent to the testing, I knew I had to meet him instead."

"And you put the manchineel fruit in his mouth." Lou's hands shook. She stepped back.

David stepped forward, smiling. "It was so much better than that. I convinced him he might need some backup, so I came with him. Once we got out of the car, I blinded him with some of the sap, then blew some ash from the burnt bark in his face. Telling him we'd been ambushed, I used one of the branches to guide him into the nursery and then forced the macerated fruit down his throat, enough that I knew it would kill him. The apple was just the cherry on top."

Eyeing the gun, Lou asked, "Not going to use a plant this time?"

David snorted out a wry laugh. "I'm not gonna kill you. I'm hoping you'll be smart enough to take the deal Harley wouldn't. Northwest Plants and I will make your silence worth your while. And what do you think Willow would feel about zero competition in the area? They can do that. I can go grab the order form I slipped under her door that proves she ordered manchineel seeds, and rip it up. She'll be off the hook. Alternately, Northwest Plants can open something new, right here in town to make it harder for her to make ends meet."

Lou's back hit the exterior fence, showing her she'd been slowly walking backward during his whole story. Her fingers gripped the chain link, the cool metal biting into her palms. She knew this nursery like the back of her hand. She could lose him.

Without overthinking it, Lou ran to her right. She flinched as David shouted and his footsteps came pounding after her. Immediately ducking to the left and hiding under a bench of vegetable starts, Lou waited, hoping he hadn't seen her.

His footsteps crunched in the other direction. Lou breathed a small sigh of relief, but it would only be a matter of time before he found her if she stayed there. Opening her text message again, she sent what she already had typed to Willow. Then immediately after, added:

David killed Harley. He has a gun!

She blinked at the screen, realizing that Willow had actually texted three times in a row before Lou had sent those last two texts.

Lou, we think David is the killer.

Hold tight. We're on our way.

Get out of there if you can.

They'd come to the same conclusion. It should've made Lou feel better, but she was still in a sticky situation. Checking the surrounding area first, Lou crawled from underneath one display table to the next. Her jeans ripped as she crawled along the concrete, small rocks biting into her palms.

She could hear David's footsteps, never far enough away for comfort.

The front gate came into view. Her car sat in the lot. Crouching low, Lou made a run for it.

A bullet whizzed past her ear.

Lou dove, hiding behind ValNur. She could see her car, but knew if she tried to run for it, he would shoot her. Just then, another bullet cracked through the air, lodging itself with a thud into ValNur's chest.

CHAPTER 24

ou kept waiting for sirens, for tires screeching, for anything that signaled help.

Willow had said they were on their way, right? Even without that, it was dinnertime in a small town, and there had just been two gunshots. Where were the town busybodies calling that in now?

One thing became certain: she couldn't stay there. David was coming toward her. Lou kept her breathing as steady as she could as she slipped back around ValNur. David's footsteps crunched as he approached the wooden troll.

Calculating her options, Lou gauged the distance to her car. Still too risky. The tiny house Willow used as an office was closer, but Lou didn't trust that she could get the key out and the lock open in time. She glanced into the nursery. In there, crowded with plants, *had* to be her safest option. She crouched low and walked along the fence just as David came around to the other side of ValNur.

"Where'd she go?" he grumbled to himself, the words biting out with a sharpness that made Lou wince.

She stepped carefully so her shoes wouldn't give her away. Sneaking back into the nursery, she ducked behind a stack of potted bamboo. It was then that she noticed the hose she'd been using to water earlier, the one she'd dropped when she'd started putting everything together.

Willow's words from last week sounded in her mind. "We have to put hoses away after watering, people. Someone could trip, and with all the pavement around here, they could get really hurt."

Lou nodded. That's what she was counting on. Just then, David came running through the aisle Lou was hiding in. She pulled the hose taut at the last moment, closing her eyes. The hose tensed as he hit it, and he let out a grunt as he flew into the air. The metal clatter of a gun told Lou he'd dropped the weapon.

Her eyes snapped open, and she quickly switched the sprayer function to the blast setting, the one Willow had also forbidden them from using. Lining it up with the gun, she blasted the weapon with a deluge of water until it skittered away, hitting the fence. Jumping up out of her hiding spot, Lou stood over the writhing body of David as he clutched his knee, skinned where he'd fallen on it. Just like he'd pointed the gun at her, she pointed the hose at him.

"Just give me a reason to soak you," she said, feeling rather like an action movie star.

Tires screeched and doors slammed as Lou's backup arrived.

"Lou! Lou?" Willow's voice was ragged as she yelled for her friend.

"In here!" Lou wanted to yell more, to give specific directions, but she'd barely been able to get out those two words before her voice cut out. The adrenaline was wearing off, and her hands were shaking so badly she wasn't sure how much longer she'd be able to hold on to the hose.

Footsteps sounded behind her, slapping against the wet pavement. Long arms wrapped around her as Willow hugged her tight, pulling her away from him as Easton and Roy raced around to arrest David.

"Gun. Over there." Lou rasped out the words, using a shaking finger to show them where it was pinned next to the fence on the wet pavement.

Easton and Roy shared a look, then glanced back at the hose Willow was prying from Lou, her fingers frozen in shock.

"You blasted the gun out of his hand with the hose?" Roy asked, sounding a little impressed.

Lou shook her head. "I tripped him."

Willow opened her arms. "See? I told everyone. The hoses are very dangerous if they're left out."

Easton chuckled. "Why don't you see if you can get something to warm Lou up. She looks like she's about to collapse."

Willow led Lou out to her office. The falsified order form David had planted sat in the doorway. Careful not to disturb it, Willow grabbed a blanket from inside and put it around Lou's shoulders, leading her to sit in the entryway as they watched the rest of the Button police force show up to help.

"He was getting desperate," Lou said, holding up the order form.

Willow read over the paper. "What was he going to do? Plant some at my house and wait until they grew to turn me in to the police?" She shook her head, unconcerned with the man and his faulty plans anymore. "What I want to know is how you figured it out."

Lou shivered, finally warming up as she told Willow about the tan lines, the throat clearing, and the second gum wrapper chain. "What about you and Easton?"

"Bella," Willow said with a sneer. "Of all people. Apparently, last night after she got home, she looked into the company emails and realized something sketchy *had* been going on. It went all the way to the top, to her parents. She found emails about someone in the Department of Agriculture letting things slide and passing them when they shouldn't have, etcetera." Willow circled her hand in front of her. "We thought she was just confirming what we'd already suspected about Harley, but then Bella said she wasn't sure how that could've been because the inside person had just emailed her dad the day prior, and Harley was dead. After that, it didn't take us long to figure out that David was a frequent visitor of a time-share in the Caribbean."

Lou swallowed. "Well, I'm glad you made it here when you did. I was out of options."

"He had a gun, Lou." Willow's expression darkened. "We heard shots. How did you survive?"

Lou peered over her shoulder at ValNur, cringing as she noticed the two bullet holes in the wooden sculpture. "ValNur saved me."

Willow sucked in a breath. "Peggy Lee was right. He is lucky."

The friends laughed together because it was so much easier than crying. Besides, everything was okay. David wouldn't be able to hurt anyone else. And Willow's nursery was finally safe.

CHAPTER 25

Two days later, Lou closed the shop for one last time. It was the *actual* grand opening of Valley Nursery.

George had made ValNur a large Medal of Honor to wear around his carved wooden neck for his valiant effort in keeping Lou alive in the face of David Houston's second attempt at murder.

Speaking of George, she was there, too, wearing Geralt as usual. The gray cat blinked up lovingly at George as she gently rested her chin on the top of his head.

Peggy Lee and Beau stood by the checkout counter, ringing up customer purchases while Willow made sure everything else was up and running. Though they wouldn't be as big of a part in the day-to-day nursery running—having their hands full working on the farm to grow the starts and plants that were harvested for the nursery—they made their appearance for the grand opening, just as had been the plan the first go-round.

Lou glanced around, frowning as she realized a few people were missing, namely Willow's parents and Easton. Ramona and Joel had come back up for the grand opening redo, and Lou was sure neither they nor Easton wanted to miss the festivities.

"Where's Easton? And your parents?" Lou asked, sidling up to Willow.

She grinned in that mischievous way that told Lou something was up. "I locked them in my office together." She hitched a thumb toward the tiny house. "I'm forcing them to be friends just like Dad did with me and Mom that time. Telling Brynn about it reminded me." She smirked. "I told them not to leave until they figure it out."

Lou's eyebrows jumped up her forehead. "That's a bold move. Do you really think—"

But Lou didn't even need to finish that question because the door to the office opened. Willow's parents and Easton stepped out of the tiny house. He and Joel shook hands, clapping one another on the back and then moving toward Willow and Lou.

"I'd say the answer is, yes. I think it worked," Willow said smugly.

The parking lot was full, customers already bustling through the space, piling plants onto carts as they shopped. The two friends sighed, looking out over the dream Willow had made into a reality.

"It's amazing, Willow," Lou said. "You really did it."

"Thanks. I couldn't have done it without you, though." Willow squeezed Lou into a side hug, beaming as she looked out over her nursery. "This is what a grand opening should look like."

Lou agreed. Nothing but plants, hard work, dreams, happiness, and not a whisker of danger to be found.

THANK YOU FOR READING!

ValNur is a "real" wooden troll at the actual Valley Nursery
in Eryn Scott's hometown.

This victim left the town of Button in *tiers*.

Button residents are normally as wary of pyramid schemes

as the next town. But when Vicki Younger comes to town promising a miracle serum, locals jump at the chance to invest in her business. When everyone loses their money and Vicki shows up dead, the town is in hot water—especially one of Lou's regulars, Silas, who was seen angrily following Vicki mere minutes before she died.

While Silas doesn't deny his anger or that he'd been shadowing Vicki, he swears he wasn't the one to end her life. Sure her friend is telling the truth, Lou asks him to recount Vicki's activities during her last hours. What Silas describes is odd to say the least, even inexplicable at times, which definitely doesn't help his plea of innocence. Can Lou untangle the clues and lead them to the true killer before Silas is put away for the rest of his days?

Buy it now!

Join Eryn Scott's mailing list to learn about new releases and sales!

STONEYBROOK MYSTERIES

Ongoing series * Farmers market * Recipes * Crime solving twins * Cats!

A MURDER AT THE MORRISEY MYSTERY SERIES

Ongoing series * Friendly ghosts * Quirky downtown Seattle building

Pebble Cove Teahouse Mysteries

Completed series * Friendly ghosts * Oregon Coast * Cat mayors

Whiskers and Words Mysteries

Ongoing series * Best friends *
Bookshop full of cats

PEPPER BROOKS
COZY MYSTERY SERIES

Completed series * Literary mysteries * Sweet romance * Cute dog

ABOUT THE AUTHOR

Eryn Scott lives in the Pacific Northwest with her husband and their quirky animals. She loves classic literature, musicals, knitting, and hiking. She writes cozy mysteries and women's fiction.

Join her mailing list to learn about new releases and sales!

www.erynscott.com

www.ingramcontent.com/pod-product-compliance
Lightning Source LLC
Chambersburg PA
CBHW021349150726
47989CB00005B/2174